DIANE CULVER

CHRISTMAS, Hamptons' Style

Hampton Thoroughbreds

Marianne –
Enjoy the Read
Diane

Palmetto Publishing Group
Charleston, SC

Christmas, Hamptons' Style

Cover photo - Robert Seifert Photography
Editor - William Coughlin

Disclaimer:
This book is a work of fiction. Names, characters, incidents, and places are a product of the author's imagination or used fictitiously. Any resemblance to persons, (living or dead), business establishments, and actual events are entirely coincidental, except for the use of Eckart's Luncheonette, which has been done with permission of the owner. The unauthorized reproduction or distribution of this copyrighted work is illegal. No part of this book can be scanned, published, or distributed in any manner without the express written consent of the author, Laurie Bumpus, writing as Diane Culver, except when quotations are embodied in articles or reviews. Thank you for respecting the author's work.

First Edition

Printed in the United States

ISBN-13: 978-1717481566
ISBN-10: 1-7174-8156-6

DEDICATION

This book is dedicated to

Shirley Eckart

A true Hampton icon and friend to all

Thank you for your love and support all these years

And for always making this author feel she is truly "HOME"

GO HURRICANES!!!!!!

PROLOGUE

July 5th
Present Day

The aroma of lavender woke Rick Stockton from a deep sleep. The strong scent tickled his nose, triggering his eyelids to flutter open only to rapidly squeeze shut. The brightness pouring in through the bedroom windows was blinding. Apparently he forgot to shut the shutters when he entered the room the previous evening.

God, his head pounded. Was someone outside drilling with a jackhammer? What he would give for his aviator sunglasses to block the sun streaming through the spotlessly clean windows. Trying to get his bearings, he slowly opened one eye and kept the other firmly shut. Counting to five, Rick opened the other and allowed it time to adjust to the glare of sunshine.

Raising his head from the pillow, he grimaced. Man, talk about a pain in the head. He scanned the room, noting it was bedecked in a nautical theme, its walls painted the color of the blue waters similar to Moriches Bay. Three surf boards of various lengths, all painted with different vertical stripes in primary colors, leaned in the corner by a white dresser. There were two hurricane lamps perched on the nightstands on each side of the king size bed. He surmised the bedside tables were made by a local craftsman, their designs carved from driftwood. A blue and white striped comforter, matching the color of the walls, lay crumpled at the foot of the bed.

Slowly righting himself, he held onto the right side of his aching head. What the hell happened? Oh, yeah.... The events of the day before rushed back. Rick's best friend, Thomas Hallock had married his sister, Courtney. The Hampton Times, no doubt, would call it the "society wedding of the year" in today's paper, and it would make page six of the New York paper as well. Thomas's mother, Helen, outdid herself to make Courtney's wedding day perfect in every way. How could he possibly ever repay her?

Well, it certainly wasn't going to be at that minute, that was for sure. For starters, he was in desperate need of a tall glass of ice water and a few aspirin for his massive hangover.

His body suddenly shivered as the south sea breeze blew in the slightly opened window by the dresser. A stabbing pain pierced his temple when he bent over to reach for the comforter. Glancing down, he saw he wore nothing more than his birthday suit. Yanking the blanket up to his chin to ward off the cold, he pivoted his head to the right. His eyes spied an unused condom lying on the night table.

Crap! I'm not that far gone to know I placed more than one there last night. Where the hell were the others?

Immediately, his eyes searched the throw rug on the floor by his side of the bed. Nothing. His heart leaped in his chest as panic set in. His eyes also roamed for his black briefs he always wore to bed. They were nowhere to be found either. Rick surveyed the room in search of his Gucci tuxedo. Lying in a trail, he spied his pants, shirt, and tie...and finally, the missing briefs. But the path didn't lead to his side of the bed, but to the other. The pillow to his left had a large indentation coupled with a few strands of light brown hair on its silk pillowcase. Trying not to jar his head, he leaned towards it, clearly smelling the lavender scent that woke him minutes ago. He'd had company.

But, who? Rick's memory was a blur and that posed one hell of a problem. Shit! Thomas is going to kill me. Rick had made a solemn promise to his best friend not to give into temptation - no one-night stands in Hampton Beach for the duration of his stay. People talk in a small town. Rick, who'd left at the age of eighteen for college, had been away from the small hamlet for twenty-two years, coming back in March to help Tom solve an embezzlement case that involved Hallock Farm's finances. Knowing Rick's passion for the ladies, Tom made a distinct point to tell him Courtney would, after the wedding, be one of the beloved Hallock clan of the village. As Tom bluntly pointed out, "Discretion was a must. Abstinence was even better." Thomas Hallock wanted nothing, NOTHING, to go awry for his new bride.

Lost in thought, Rick hadn't heard the pounding on the cottage door, but when a familiar voice called his name, he snapped to attention.

"Richard! Richard! Are you in there?"

Judas Priest! No! No! Please, let me dig a hole and jump right in it this instant.

On the other side of the door was the voice of Helen Hallock, matriarch of the prestigious Hallock family, and Tom's mother. "Richard Preston Stockton! I know you're in there. Thomas told me you slept out here because the house was full of family." The knocking became louder and more persistent. "I swear you're just like my boys. I should put you over my knee and spank you. Open the door this minute! You left your coat in the main house at the after party. It's has been ringing all morning!"

My coat! Suddenly realizing the jacket was not part of the trail of clothing, he hopped out of bed. This time he didn't care how much his head hurt. Rick threw on what clothes he did have and made himself somewhat presentable. "I'm coming!" he called out. "Give me a minute to get decent, Mrs. H."

With his pants on and his shirt half buttoned, he quickly flung the comforter over the bed, hoping it would seem as if he'd slept in the large bed solo during the night.

Opening the door, his eyes were hit with an even brighter ray of light. Squinting, he motioned for the elder woman to enter.

Helen gave him a once over as she walked in the door. "You certainly looked like you partied way too much as well." She nodded her head in the direction of the main house. "A few who managed to get out of bed are drinking Bloody Marys in the dining room. Hannah is having a fit since she took great care to make a beautiful brunch. No one wants to remotely touch the food!" The elder woman's shoulders shook as she burst out laughing.

Rick had come to know her well in the last four months. She was relishing every minute seeing him in his present state. Her chuckle echoed in the small quarters adding to the pain in his head. He winced, replying, "Food sounds good, Mrs. H. But you mentioned something about my coat ringing? That's my phone. Beats me why I left it behind. With my business, I always clip it on my belt. I haven't the faintest idea how it wound up in my coat pocket."

Being six foot two, he towered over her. Glancing down, he spied a devil-like twinkle in her eyes. Beware. *The lady's got something to say.*

She cleared her throat and pointed to his pants. "Richard, you are not wearing your belt nor do I see it anywhere on the floor." Her eyes made a pass over the contents of the small room. "And what is that smell? It's so – so - rich." She paused as her nose sniffed the air. Glancing up at him, she stated, "Why, it's lavender." Helen's voice purred like a kitten.

Okay, so she knows I had a visitor. There's no way I'm going to grovel and try to wheedle out of her of all people who it might have been. If I did that, whatever I did last night would be all over town and she'd be planning another wedding. Mine.

Fingers snapped in front of his face rousing him from his musings. "Now, young man. Get your clothes together. You promised Thomas you'd have everyone's tuxes put together for Hannah to take to the dry cleaner by noon. I know you'll take yours back with you. Promise me you'll get something to eat before you jet out of here." She wagged her finger in front of his face. "I won't take no for an answer. Robert and I truly wish you could stay longer, but we understand you have to get back to your job in New York."

Being gentlemanly, Rick opened the door, hoping she'd take the hint and depart. "I promise. First, though, I think I need a shower and a shave to make myself a bit more presentable. How does thirty minutes sound? I'll grab a small bite and tend to the tuxedos. I apologize for having to be on my way so quickly. Thanks for bringing me my coat and phone. I still can't fathom how it got left at the main house. Maybe I was too hot at the after party and took my coat off and stuffed the phone in my pocket." He scratched his chin. "I always carry it 24/7."

Helen wrapped him in a big motherly bear hug and whispered in his ear. "Well, I'm certainly not puzzled by why. You're just going to have to figure that out for yourself." As she stepped out onto the deck of the cottage overlooking the Thoroughbred horse farm, Thomas's mother turned back to face him, her deep blue eyes pierced his. "I think you better start with that white note lying on the night stand on the other side of your bed." She winked, turned, and strode quickly down a gravel path that led to the back door of the main house.

Note? What note? The woman had eyes like a hawk. He hadn't seen anything, but heck he hadn't seen straight since he first woke up. Sure enough, when he reentered the cottage, he spied a tiny card propped up on the hurricane lamp. Picking it up, he saw the imprinting of a blank RSVP card to the wedding on one side. That's why I missed it. I thought it was my invitation.

Turning the crème colored card over, he read what was written in bold lettering.

LAST NIGHT WAS A BIG, BIG MISTAKE!!
DON'T CALL ME.........EVER!!!!!

It was then the hazy fog that surrounded his brain lifted. The bold cursive writing he'd read so often throughout Tom's case suddenly registered. He'd spent the night with the woman he'd fallen in love with from the minute they crossed swords. However, the message on the card was meant to make things perfectly clear to him regarding their night together.

Rick had news for Sarah Adams. He'd find her. He had to. Something had obviously gone amiss since she hadn't woken up beside him. He was desperate to know why. Thomas and the entire Hallock clan would make mincemeat out of him if they were to find out what transpired between him and their beloved "adopted daughter/sister". However, it wasn't going to be an easy task. The woman worked as a CIA operative, but used the "manager" of the local beach club as her cover. Should she decide to play hide and seek, he, too, had an arsenal of investigative resources to put to good use. By Christmas, with luck on his side, Rick was determined the lady would be his.

CHAPTER ONE

Eckart's Luncheonette
Hampton Beach, Long Island
September 5th

"Excuse me. Pardon me." Sarah Adams worked her way to the head of the line attempting to get inside the overcrowded restaurant. What were all these people doing here? It never took her fifteen minutes to find a parking place. Ever. Even in the summer. Had she known the place was going to be hopping, she'd have ridden her bike from her new apartment on Jessup Lane.

When her phone rang at five that morning, with a ringtone of a Frank Sinatra tune registering in her subconscious, Sarah moaned. She pulled the covers over her head and let the call go to voice mail three times. However, the caller was persistent. Knowing she'd never get an ounce of peace and curious as to why she was being called at the crack of dawn, she picked up the phone, pressed the "accept" button, and growled, "What. Is. It."

It was that five-minute conversation that had her standing in the doorway of Eckart's, barely awake and yawning from overwhelming fatigue. A hand waved in the air, beckoning her to the back corner booth of the iconic Hampton landmark. Sarah waved an acknowledgement in return.

From the time she'd come back to Hampton Beach, Sarah learned that when Shirley Eckart called, you answered. If she said come, you did. No questions asked. And she had been summoned, wondering why it was imperative to arrive "at the stroke of nine". Was she going to be cast in some sort of reality version of Hampton Cinderella? Knowing Mrs. E. was part of the infamous Hampton Beach matchmaking trio of Helen Hallock, and Helen's sister-in-law, Elizabeth, the Director of the CIA, Sarah's radar immediately pinged to the "on" position. Pray you're mistaken, she thought to herself.

Having thrown on the clothes closest to her bed along with a Hurricanes baseball cap, she pulled the brow of the hat low over her brow. The seats at the counter were filled with "townies", all perched on their assigned seats. Everyone in town, even the summer people, knew *NOT* to mess with the counter stools. You earned the right to sit there and God help you if you sat where you didn't belong. As she made her to the back of the luncheonette, the old-timers called out a morning greeting. She touched the brim of her cap as she passed by.

Sliding into the booth, Sarah was met with a warm, gracious smile. Mrs. E. was always up beat. It was one of the things Sarah loved most about her. "Good morning, sunshine." The woman's smile quickly turned into a frown. "My word, girl. You look like hell."

"And good morning to you." Sarah had no time for idle chit-chat. "You didn't let me get a word in edgewise and give me a chance to bring up the fact I was sleeping in. Me and the other employees almost passed out when Matt announced he was giving us today off. He closed the beach club! I had every intention of sleeping until noon…until you called at five a.m.!" Sarah crossed her arms over her George Washington sweatshirt and stared down the woman seated across from her. "Then, my plans included unpacking the mountain of boxes from my move and attempting to settle into my new abode. I should have known something would come up." Sarah muttered under her breath, "Nothing's been going right lately."

"What? What do you…"

Sarah had no intention of explaining why she cut off Mrs. E. "Nothing. You were saying?"

The woman placed her silverware on the table and placed a napkin in her lap. "I still can't believe you left that beautiful apartment above the German deli on Main Street. Have you any idea how many people would pay to have a view of the canal and be able to dock their boat for free? Besides, you enjoyed being able to paddle your kayak up and down the canal to the marina after a long day at work. You said it was cathartic."

"Well, this apartment came with free rent for a year if I house-sit for Stan and Peggy Whitman." Mrs. E. stared back at Sarah, a perplexed look crossed her face. "You know. The movie director and his wife, the fashion designer, the one with the boutique shop on Main Street. Plus, it's in a perfect location, just over Jessup Bridge. I can bike to work and get some exercise and even be in town within five minutes now that the summer crowd has left. I'm going to take the rent money and help my grandparents pay their assisted living bills."

Surprised, Mrs. E. countered, "I didn't realize there were money problems."

"No, they're fine. Really." Sarah spoke in a whisper. "I would just feel better knowing there's a slush fund of money in the bank should the need arise. Pop wasn't as savy as Gram when it came to keeping tabs on their savings."

"But, what about you? Matt must pay you well for being his manager. Don't you need to be setting aside money for a rainy day for your retirement?"

Always the worrier. Mrs. E. didn't know everything...for good reason. Sarah was born and raised until the age of seven in Hampton Beach. When her parents completed their PhDs at Stony Brook, they moved upstate to take jobs teaching in their respective fields at Syracuse University. Sarah graduated from a small high school on the outskirts of the small city. Due to her tremendous academic and athletic success, she accepted a full scholarship to George Washington University. There she majored in criminal justice with a minor in art history. Three weeks after her graduation, while Sarah was backpacking through Europe, her parents were killed in a horrific car crash while on holiday touring the East Coast.

Devastated and not knowing whom to turn to besides her grandparents, word spread through the small hamlet that she was in need of a job ASAP. To this day, she was eternally grateful to Thomas's aunt, Elizabeth, for reaching out. Elizabeth Hallock told her she'd followed Sarah during her time spent in D.C., especially the internships she took part in within the nation's justice system. The Director offered her a spot at the Farm, the CIA training facility. Sarah readily accepted, graduating at the top of her class. For the following seven years, Sarah risked life and limb in the European theater before getting shot on her last assignment in London. Her minor in art history came in handy in three cases on the continent. Forced to return to D.C. and report back to Langley, she earned high praise from the lady in charge.

After doing desk duty for several months an opening for an agent occurred on Long Island. Sarah jumped at the chance to be close to home, set down roots, and still perform what she was trained to do. No one in town knew her other than the beach club's manager, except for the closely-knit inner circle of the Hallock family.

With her expenses paid in full by the Agency during the time on the job, she'd amassed a significant amount of wealth by investing wisely, thanks to the advice from Elizabeth's second in command, Sam Tanner. Sarah could live on that money for years to come should she choose to do so. But sitting on her butt wasn't her style.

Mrs. E.'s hand waved in front of her face. "Hey! You still with me?"

Shocked she'd drifted off, and chagrined at being caught, she hung her head. "Sorry. That's been happening a lot lately. If my head hits the table and I'm out cold just roll me into your car and take me home. I feel as if I could sleep until Halloween and never wake up." Her effort to smile failed.

Eyeing Sarah curiously, her breakfast companion replied, "This isn't like you. You're always at the top of your game." Mrs. E. stopped talking as a waitress placed plates of food on the table. "I took the liberty and ordered our usual."

Sarah took one whiff of the chocolate chip pancakes and was immediately hit with a wave of nausea. Taking a deep breath, she swallowed, hoping her stomach wouldn't react as it had the past several weeks. Lately, all she could manage to keep down was strong Earl Grey tea, wheat toast, and an occasional toasted English muffin.

"What's the matter? Don't you want breakfast?" When Sarah looked up, the woman's hazel eyes were scrutinizing her from top to bottom. Shirley's hand slapped the table. "I knew it. You're sick."

Sarah vehemently shook her head. "No." She crossed her fingers beneath the table. How she hated to lie. "I've been trying to cut down on the really heavy carbs and do away with the caffeine."

"Baloney. Out with it." The woman sat back and crossed her arms over her breasts. "Listen, I was a mother. Something's bothering you and messing with your health." She reached across the table, taking Sarah's left hand in hers. "Have you been to see Doc Davis?"

"No. I probably should go. I'm so fatigued and don't have an appetite. I cry at the drop of a hat. Frankly, I'm afraid to see him. Maybe something's seriously wrong."

"Just a minute... Clara!" Mrs. E. called to the waitress who was cleaning up the next table and instructed her to take away the food. "Bring a mug of decaf tea and some lightly buttered toast for Sarah. I'll just drink my coffee." She turned back for Sarah's approval. "How's that?"

"Perfect. Thanks." There was no way she was going to tell the woman, who she considered a second mother, what she'd been living on for two weeks. Drawing in a deep breath to steady her nerves, Sarah stated, "I'll call and make an appointment. I hope I can get in with it being a holiday week and all. Doc might be on vacation."

Mrs. E. responded, "Doc never takes a vacation. You'll get in. If you have a problem you call me."

Needing to change the subject, Sarah asked, "So why the early morning call? What's going on? This place is rocking."

Shirley leaned back, shocked. "Sarah Adams! You've lived in Hampton Beach for four years. Don't tell me you've forgotten what day this is?"

Sarah merely shrugged her shoulders. "Beats me."

"Girl, it's Tumbleweed Tuesday! You know? Our townie celebration that all the summer people have returned to their luxurious apartments and condos in New York City."

"You brought me here for that?" Sarah rested her elbows on the table and put her head in her hands. Out of the corner of her eye she saw Clara returning with a hot cup of tea and toast as directed. She leaned back in her seat letting the waitress place the food before her. She nodded her thanks, getting a smile in return. *At least somebody's happy this morning.* She continued, "I could be home in bed. Do you know how many days I've had off in four years? *One.*" Sarah stuck her index finger in the air to emphasize the fact. As she was trying to make her point about being dragged from her cozy bed, she watched as the woman took a small envelope from her lap and placed it on the table next to her own cup.

"Now, listen to me, young lady." Mrs. E.'s voice was firm, but motherly. "I've had this feeling in my gut you haven't gone to the Post Office lately. When was the last time you checked your mailbox?"

Mailbox? Post Office? *For this I got out of a nice warm bed? Just play along. She'll get to the point soon and you can go home.* "Uh…I pay most of my bills online. I guess, to answer your question, it's been close to three weeks. Why?"

Taking a good look at the large envelope Mrs. E. held in her hand, she zoomed in on a black "H" engraved on its back.

Chills shot up her arms. *Oh no. Please, please, don't let it be what I think it is.*

Mrs. E. handed the fancy stationary across the table. "Read it."

Sarah had no choice but to take the fancy envelope into her hands and withdraw the contents. It resembled a wedding invitation. When she opened the inner envelope, she was confused in that it was an invitation to another Hallock gala. Sarah read the card carefully, not understanding why it had anything to do with her.

You are cordially invited to
attend the baptism of John Christopher Clinton, Jr.

ST. MARK'S CHURCH
40 MAIN STREET
HAMPTON BEACH, NY 11978

SEPTEMBER 30TH
TIME: 2 P.M.

Reception to follow immediately after

HAMPTON BEACH COUNTRY CLUB
RETURN RSVP CARD BY SEPTEMBER 14TH

She summarized what she read out loud. "So Kate and John are bringing the new baby from Virginia to be baptized. They did the same thing with little Lizzie." Finished, she replaced the card into its envelope and returned it.

"It's going to be a grand event. You know how Helen operates." Mrs. E. beamed like the Cheshire Cat.

Deciding to play along, she said, "Yes, Mrs. H. does know how to throw a party. But, what's that," she waggled her forefinger at the invitation, "got to do with me?"

"Boy, for being so smart, you sure are dense. Do I have to spell it out? You're like family to the Hallocks. There's no doubt you've received an invite as well. Talking to Helen over the last few weeks, I found out she invited one very special guest. Someone, especially you, if I'm not mistaken, might like to see again." Gleefully, the excited woman clapped her hands together, like a kid seeing presents under the tree on Christmas morning.

Sarah hated to put a damper on the woman's elation. She took a deep sip of her tea, hoping Mrs. E. was wrong. Trying to mask her trembling voice, she asked, "And who might that be?" For some unknown reason, her body started to shake, dreading what she'd already assumed, but didn't want to hear.

Mrs. E. slowly rose and came to crouch next to her and gently laid a hand upon Sarah's knee. "Who do you think? Rick Stockton! We saw you two at the wedding. The way you danced and talked, your heads close together. You two spent the entire night in each other's company." Sarah, who was drinking her tea, started to choke and placed her mug on the table. No. The woman couldn't possibly know what happened after the after party. "The two of you were downright cozy. Oh, Sarah. When Rick put his arm around you during the fireworks and hugged you to his side, I just knew he was the man for you. You must be thrilled to think there's a chance you could see him again. No?"

Shell-shocked and feeling as if she'd been sucker-punched, Sarah was speechless. She jumped up from her seat, almost knocking Mrs. E. over in the process. There was only one place she needed to go. "How much do I owe you for breakfast?"

"Oh, honey. It's on the house. Go." She shooed Sarah out the door, calling out, "Jog down to Main. It's not worth trying to find a parking space. The townies are happy to..."

Sarah didn't hear the last of what Mrs. E. had to say. Closing the wooden door behind her, she was glad she'd donned her shorts, sweatshirt and running shoes. Out on the sidewalk, she briefly stopped to draw in a breath of fresh air. She had to steady her nerves before she faced the inevitable. Turning left, she sprinted down Mill Road past Follett's Funeral Home. It didn't take long to arrive at her destination. Within a few minutes, she was racing up the granite steps of the imposing, brick building.

Retrieving the multitude of mail from her post box, she rummaged through the pile. Pulling out what looked as if it might be the invitation, she laid the unimportant papers on a nearby table. Gingerly, she opened the envelope.

There, written in bold, black calligraphy, was her worst nightmare – the invitation to the baptism. An image of her of lying naked with Rick ready to enter her flashed through her mind. Just thinking of that mere image sent a tingling between her legs, forcing her to squeeze them together. Her mind was a blur from the images of all he had done to her that night and into the early morning hours before the sun came up.

Now was the moment of truth. Should she mark "yes" or "no" on the RSVP? Mrs. E. was correct. No matter what she wrote in the note she left by the bed, that night had proved, in no uncertain terms, Rick *was* her Mr. Right, as much as she so desperately wanted to deny it. In the three months they'd worked side by side, butting heads the majority of the time, he'd grown on her. She scoffed at her friends who believed in love at first sight. But, somehow, some way, it had happened… to her.

The note she left by the bedside gave her the justification to simply mark "no". She could walk away and never face Rick again. If she didn't appear, he'd no doubt get the message… again.

Sarah possessed a strong faith and morals. She wasn't a woman who did one-night stands. In fact, she never had one… EVER! She believed in love, marriage and family, in that order. From what she ascertained in their brief time working together on Operation Hallock Farm, their values and personalities were so dissimilar. And in her playbook, opposites didn't attract. Why draw out the agony?

But Sarah was also pragmatic. She wouldn't be satisfied unless she saw things through, whether the outcome is good or bad. A "yes" was her chance to look the man in the eye, without any alcohol to impede her inhibitions, and find out if "Mr. One-Night Stand" had showed her his true soul that night on the Fourth of July. Would he tell her again she was unlike any other woman he'd ever met?

Hell, it was imperative she knew how he felt, considering what she might be facing. Why? Because the events of her life had denied her time to find her one true, everlasting love. March had "roared in like a lion" with Rick Stockton in tow. He wasn't a figment of her imagination. Was it too much to ask for Love, Hamptons' Style?

CHAPTER TWO

Two weeks earlier
New York City

Dressed in a navy blue Armani suit, white shirt and yellow tie, Rick Stockton stood, his hands in the pockets of his pants, viewing the New York City skyline. His business, Stockton Investigative Enterprises, comprised the top three floors of the prestigious Madison Avenue skyscraper. Looking out the thirty-fourth floor window of his corner office, he applauded his good fortune at the business's exponential growth. It had been eight years since he picked up and moved his operations from Washington, D.C.

Having done free-lance work with the NSA, FBI and CIA, he was fortunate to tap into a pool of workers who were more than glad to join him in his foray to the Big Apple. Once established, he found he had more cases than he and his team could handle. Once the word was out his firm was in search of a multitude of top-level employees, with different investigative skill sets, his initial D.C. staff of ten people exploded to one hundred and twenty. On the advice of his best friend's aunt, Elizabeth Hallock, who presently served as the Director of the CIA, his firm "crossed the pond" opening small satellite offices in London, Paris and Rome.

A small town boy gone global, Rick never took for granted all his success afforded him. Growing up, he, his sister, and parents were nothing more than "townies" in the village of Hampton Beach. It was there, in seventh grade, during a food fight in the school's cafeteria, he came face to face with Thomas Hallock, the eldest son of the wealthy Hallock family. Anyone would have thought the two boys would forever be at odds with each other, coming from different sides of the tracks, but on that particular day they became fast friends. Rick was proud back then to call Tom his "adopted" brother. Now, since Thomas's recent marriage to Rick's sister, Courtney, he'd gained a brother-in-law.

Ignoring the stack of papers piled high on his desk, he stared out the window, his mind sixty miles to the east, immersed in memories of a night spent in a small cottage on the back of the Hallock Farm property. His dreams haunted him since that fateful night when he bedded Sarah Adams. After reading the note she left on the side of the bed, he tried everything in his power to contact her. It was imperative she know that night meant the world to him. To her, he did not want to be "Mr. One-Night Stand" as he was so often referred to in the tabloids.

With his secretary thinking he was diligently at work, he felt he could spare a few more minutes to think of the tanned, lithe and athletically built woman. Upon his arrival to work Operation Hallock Farm, Sarah was introduced to him as the manager of the Sunfish Beach Club. A week into the investigation there came a need to add a member to his team, one who could blend among the people in the different hamlets. Rick, still to this day, could not believe the shock that washed over him, during a classified briefing at the Fox Hollow Inn, when Sarah strolled in. Literally, he almost fell out of his chair. Speechless, he was stunned to learn Sarah, like his sister, Courtney, was a CIA operative. Her eyes immediately locked onto his. Her body language and demeanor told him she wasn't pleased at being summoned. Parking herself in the vacant chair beside him, she leveled a dagger-like glare in his direction. And the "fun" had begun.

Rick started to pace the Oriental carpet in his office. He withdrew his hands from his pockets and ran his fingers through his hair. His mind was in turmoil, trying to separate the thoughts of their working relationship with those leading up to of the night of July Fourth, the day of Courtney's wedding to Thomas.

Sarah was indeed feisty. From the time spent with her on the case, he concluded she was a true patriot. It was obvious she'd been trained by the best. However, when things didn't go her way – watch out. If he said "black", she countered "white". They clashed from the get-go. Throughout the three short months it took to bring the sting to fruition, his admiration and respect for her drive and determination grew. Her ability to stay focused and deliver the outcomes on the tasks given her, some extremely dangerous, impressed him beyond measure. And somewhere, in the middle of everything, he realized Sarah Adams was "the one".

Rick fell hard. That much he knew. Never, ever, in his life had he experienced the sense of longing to be with a woman as he did with Sarah. He was closing in on forty. It had been his objective to take on a partner in his business when the operation came to a close. Rick couldn't keep up with the rigors of being CEO. Nor did he want to any longer. His thought that Courtney would readily join his firm came crashing down on him when she announced she was in love with Tom and they'd be married on the Fourth of July. As his sister succinctly put it, "My life of living a fast paced, dangerous life is over. Come to think of it, brother, you should do the same." Her words had stunned him, as he'd always pictured her a career CIA agent much like Tom's aunt. But one day, seeing how Courtney and Thomas interacted, he knew she'd found the Mr. Right she'd been searching for, the man her job had never let her find. Rick was sad to see his personal plan tank, but he truly couldn't be happier for his sister.

With their parents deceased, it fell to Rick to take on the traditional roles of mother and father of the bride. Now, six weeks after the wedding, his throat still clogged up remembering how radiant and happy Courtney had looked as he walked her down the aisle of St. Mark's Church, the train of her Vera Wang wedding dress trailing behind her. By the end of the brother-sister dance, he needed to withdraw the red handkerchief from his tuxedo pocket in order to dab away the tears rolling down his cheeks.

Waking up in an empty bed the morning after his sister's nuptials, surrounded by the smell of lavender, Rick still couldn't recall much about his night with Sarah. He, like Courtney, knew without a shadow of a doubt that he'd found the only person he wanted by his side forever. Sarah Adams was a rare beauty in mind, body and soul. He stopped at the edge of the rug and looked out towards the East River. He wanted Sarah. He needed her. He loved her, damn it! But – was she as much in the dark about their night together? No, he had to believe she knew what had happened. Why ever would she have left that note? Rick wasn't an expert, but people couldn't possibly share the kind of passion and chemistry and not be vested in some form. No, Sarah had feelings for him. He was positive on that score.

Feeling anger building from within, Rick thought of the last six weeks and his attempts to make contact with her. Matt answered the phone at the beach club stating flatly, "She not here." or "She's down on the beach doing her job." He gave up calling her cell. She ignored his calls. Even Helen Hallock was wary when he called to ask for the Director's private home phone number. The elder woman resisted at first, but finally relented.

Thinking that the number one matchmaker in the country would not turn him down and help him, he was taken aback by the Director's curt reply. Elizabeth Hallock put him his place.

"Rick, you do *not* have an international crisis on your hands. For heaven's sake, you have resources. Use them! You do operate an investigative agency the last I heard." He detected a slight hint of a chuckle at the other end of the line before she'd promptly hung up the phone.

Running his finger through his hair once more, he glanced down at the Rolex on his wrist. Yikes! He'd drifted off into another world for forty minutes. His secretary was more than likely in her office wondering what was taking so long. The thing he loved the most about Mary Winston was the fact she ran his business like clockwork.

Rick was determined not to give up. There had to be a way to find Sarah and make her see they were meant to be together. For all he knew, the townies were gossiping about "Mr. One-Night Stand" and she'd gone into hiding. Or worse, Elizabeth had sent her out on assignment somewhere to some God forsaken part of the world. But Matt would never state, "She's working down on the beach." if that had truly been the case. Were they all in collusion to keep her whereabouts unknown? Had she told Courtney and the clan to close ranks?

Rick had to convince Sarah the night they made love, coupled with whatever he said and did, was when he was certain he truly loved her, madly and deeply. For richer, for poorer, for better or worse. Being a person whose job it was to find a needle in a haystack, he was doing one lousy job locating the woman of his dreams.

CHAPTER THREE

"Ahem! Rick!" A loud, feminine voice snapped Rick out of his daydreams. As he turned from the floor to ceiling windows, he faced his secretary. Standing on the opposite side of his desk, Mary stood staring at him, a bewildered expression on her face. "You were miles away. I tried to get your attention three times. Is there something you'd care to share? I'm here for you, you know."

Mary had been an integral part of his business since his days in D.C. She reminded him of a softer, maternal version of Elizabeth Hallock. However, there was no way he was going to tell the older woman his present tale of woe.

"Sorry. Just a few things on my mind." He walked to his desk and sat down in the brown, leather chair. As he made himself comfortable, he spread out the papers he was supposed to have signed over an hour ago. "I appreciate your concern, though. Thanks for asking." What was the sin in telling a little white lie? "Mary, to be honest, my mind is on my sister. I've been wondering how to see her more often. Lately, work always gets in the way." He paused, picked up a pen from his desk and glanced up. Mary eyed him suspiciously. He surmised the woman hadn't believed one word he'd said. "You must be here for the documents. Let me just glance them over. It shouldn't take more than thirty minutes to sign them."

Without an invitation to do so, he watched Mary park herself in one of the two chairs that faced him. This was definitely a first. Always one for proper office protocol, she never assumed to sit without first asking permission to do so. Oh, boy. The lady had something on her mind. Mary cocked her head, her gaze curious. "That would be perfect," she replied. "The papers must be faxed overseas by tomorrow morning for the London office."

Understanding that time was of the essence and he had procrastinated way too long, he glanced down and started to quickly read, signing each of the sheets of paper. He expected, once he began, Mary would leave. But she stayed put. She had subtle ways of attracting his attention when something was on her mind besides business. "Can I get you coffee? You look as if you could use a 'pick me up'."

The woman read his mind. "Think there's any Baileys around?" Both parties smiled, knowing the habit he'd picked up from his time spent on his last case in the Hamptons. There wasn't a Hallock who didn't start the day without adding a nip of the Irish liqueur into a cup of tea or coffee. And it had to be Baileys. Period. "No sugar and cream. Just black. I really hate to ask you to wait on me knowing there's a perfectly good working Keurig machine in the staff room. If you don't mind getting me a cup, it would help me whittle down this pile a whole lot faster."

Mary grinned. It seemed as if she was trying her best to stifle a laugh. "That last assignment really changed you into an honorary Hallock, didn't it? Let me see what I can rustle up." She pointed to his desk blotter. "Read those papers and put your John Hancock on the bottom."

"Yes, ma'am. Sounds like a plan."

Mary rose and walked to the door. Once there, she turned and called over her shoulder. "By the way. I may have the perfect solution to that dilemma you were mulling over when I walked in."

The pen he held slipped from his fingers and landed on the desk. Rick leveled a questioning gaze at his secretary. "I haven't the faintest idea what you're referring to. There is no 'dilemma'." He made quotation marks with his fingers.

"Yes. Right. And I'm the Queen of England." Mary wagged her forefinger at him. "You can't get that Sarah Adams out of your mind. Don't deny it. You've been distracted by something that happened with her since you returned to the city." She winked as if she knew his secret. "I'll be back in a few minutes."

As she walked out the door, Rick could swear the woman was humming "Here Comes the Bride" under her breath.

* * *

Fifteen minutes later, Mary stood by his side, her hand out for the signed business documents. Everything was meticulously done to his specifications. His coffee sat on a tray she placed on his desk. Rick found it difficult to concentrate on the papers before him since Mary walked away announcing she come up with a "solution".

Mary reminded him of three older women he'd come to know well during his time spent in Hampton Beach. Adding a fourth woman to the infamous mix would be a lethal combination and would spell trouble with a capital T. When she'd been retrieving his coffee, he wondered if he should tell her what happened, bring her into his confidence. But in all honesty, he was afraid of her reaction. However, on the other hand, acting in the official capacity as his secretary she might be able to help him get through to Mrs. Eckart, Helen, and Elizabeth for help in his search to contact Sarah. What did he have to lose? His gut told him to put on the brakes. He had to give that particular option more thought.

"There." Rick signed the last document, flexing his hand, and sliding the stack of white papers into an eight by ten manila folder. He handed the large envelope to Mary. "Thank you. I know I put the staff on a very strict deadline."

"That's why you pay them so well." Instead of making for the door, she walked around his desk and, once again, sat down. His sixth sense told him she had something important to share.

Rick watched as she withdrew a piece of paper from a fancy envelope. She'd hidden it beneath the larger envelope she carried in. Tapping its corner on the edge of his desk, she pursed her lips. Her dark brown eyes locked onto his. "One more thing, if I may?"

Cautiously, he replied, "You may." His eyes were glued to what she held in her hand.

"I would normally answer this sort of correspondence, but I felt this... particular invitation," she waved the white envelope before him, "needs your personal attention."

Wondering what Mary could possibly be referring to, Rick was intrigued. He reached for his cup of coffee and brought it to his lips, taking a deep swallow. His eyes never left Mary. Licking his lips, he first replied, "Ah...Baileys. Thank you."

Mary politely answered, "I've given specific instructions there be a bottle on hand. I'm sure there's some story why everyone needs to drink it. But right now, I need your full attention, Richard Preston Stockton."

This wasn't going to be good, he thought. No one but his sister and Helen Hallock, called him by his full name, and only when he crossed the line. He couldn't imagine what he'd done to Mary, so he gave her his undivided attention.

She eyed him warily. "You've made it perfectly clear over the years how much you detest going out and about to certain social events in the city. You've had me decline 'for business reasons', but you and I both know that's not the case. You always see to your own..." she hesitated, clearing her throat, "...personal calendar." The woman blushed. Rick squirmed in his seat knowing exactly what she was alluding to. "This..." she waved the crème colored envelope in front of him, "came a few days ago. I wrestled with what I should do. After seeing you staring out those windows, I'm certain now, more than ever, it does deserve your personal RSVP." She handed the cardboard stock paper to Rick and sat back, regal as a queen, her hands folded demurely in her lap.

Taking the invitation in hand, Rick read the contents, then read it once more. His brow furrowed and he glanced up for clarification. "Why would I want to go to Kate and John's son's baptism? I've never been invited to other family functions. Well, other than my sister's wedding."

His secretary let out a disgusted sigh. Bracing himself for what might be headed his way, he leaned back in his chair.

"Richard. I've made a *huge* attempt not to interfere in your personal life."

There it was again. Richard. What was it about this invite that made it different from all the others? He wasn't seeing the connection. "I appreciate how you've always handled my social calendar, Mary. But, why should I go? Do your usual. Pick out a gift and I'll pen a short note like I always do. There's too much on my plate here at the office. Besides, I may need to be in London to go over the financial fallout from that art heist four days after the baptism. I won't have much time to ready my team for the trip, so, as you can see, this clearly doesn't fit into my work schedule."

As his words trailed off, he spotted "the look" on Mary's face. There had to be a major reason for attending this event. "You, Richard, are being invited due to the fact your sister is now part of Hampton society. As her brother, like it or not, you're viewed as family ever since Courtney married Thomas."

"I truly understand they want to include me. Really, I do. And it's very nice of them to think of me. But tell them I'm sorry. That my business in London will more than likely take me out of the States."

"Honest to goodness. You're entirely missing the point." Mary threw her hands in the air. The large manila envelope in her lap floated to the floor. Frustration was written all over her face.

Was that the sound of a stamping foot on the other side of his desk? Rick eyed her quizzically. "Listen, I'm late for a meeting with my IT team. What exactly am I not getting?"

Mary rubbed her hands together, leaned closer and whispered as if she were imparting classified information. "My sources in the Hallock inner circle tell me the one and only one Sarah Adams was also issued an invitation!" His eyebrows arched in surprise at the revelation, but he tried to remain stoic. Mary continued, "The rumor mill says she'll have every excuse in the book for not wanting to go… just like you. However, I know for a fact someone's going to convince her otherwise. Sarah's not going to have a choice." She paused, looking as pleased as punch, then continued, "You know I hear things out at my desk. I don't mean to eavesdrop, mind you, but you've been trying to reach that woman for six weeks. Haven't you?" She crossed her arms across her ample bosom, a triumphant look on her face. "And don't you dare deny you weren't thinking about her when I walked in here. I'd bet my year-end bonus on it."

His jaw sagged at the woman's astuteness. Or was she a damn good psychic? He picked up his pen to ready his response. Not wanting to sound overly eager, he asked, "Well, what do you think? Is Sarah really going to show?"

His secretary bent over and retrieved the large envelope from the floor. Rick didn't see the woman cross her fingers beneath it. "Absolutely. Shirley Eckart assured everyone to leave it up to her that Sarah will be there. Trust me. Shirley has a way of being, how shall I put it...persuasive. Mark my words. Your Sarah will come."

He liked the sound of those words. His Sarah. He could envision it all now. Their first date, followed by visiting him in New York. Nights out on the town. A proposal on one knee at the top of the Empire State Building. Whoa! Where had he conjured up those thoughts?

First, he had to get the lady back, because things apparently ended on the downturn from the tone of the note she'd left. He picked up the card and marked the RSVP card in the affirmative and scribbled a short note on the bottom. Looking across the desk, he saw a broad smile on his secretary's face. He handed the card to Mary after sealing the envelope shut.

"See that the RSVP gets out in the afternoon mail," he instructed. "You better be right or I'm going to look like a damn fool." This time it was Rick who shook his forefinger at Mary. "And you, dear secretary, will be out a boat load of money come the end of the year!"

"Trust me on this, boss. My sources are good." Mary sounded like a secret agent. She rose from her seat, manila and RSVP envelopes in hand. She walked to his office door. "Open or closed?"

"Closed, please. I've got things to do." The door was almost shut when he called out, "Wait!" Enthused at the thought of seeing Sarah, Rick had forgot to ask Mary for one more thing.

Mary opened the door wider. "Yes?"

"Forget what I said about your choosing the gift. I'll pick out my own. Can you get me a Tiffany's catalog?" From the look on Mary's face, he thought she was about to faint dead away from shock.

The woman recovered quickly, a twinkle of delight appeared in her eyes. "Yes, sir!" She saluted as she went out the door.

Feeling like a teenager who just received a "yes" when he'd asked the girl of his dreams to the prom, Rick spun his leather chair around and around, pumping his fists in the air. Finally! A second chance to show Sarah how perfect they'd be together, that opposites really do attract. And, more importantly, he had to fix whatever made her flee from his bed, instead of waking up beside him.

Putting his thoughts on hold, he hit the intercom button. "Mary?"

"Yes?" Was the woman's voice actually purring?

"Cancel my four o'clock and ask my driver to pick me up at four-thirty."

"Yes, right away." Click.

Rick stood up and walked over to one more take in the view from his window, this time filled with far more optimism than before. He chuckled at the thought of the salesperson at Tiffany's and her delight when she'd ring up his purchases on his silver platinum AMBANK card - a silver rattle for the new Clinton baby. And, for good measure, he'd pick out a four-carat diamond ring for his lady. What had Tom told him? One always had to be ready to do it up right – Hamptons' Style!

CHAPTER FOUR

The Wellness Clinic
Riverhead, Long Island
September 12th

Shelby Connor, Doc's long-time physician's assistant, took Sarah's vitals: weight, blood pressure and temperature, recording the results on the paper she placed on the counter.

"So. Sarah?" The woman glanced up from her writing, a bright smile on her face. "What brings you in to see Doc today? The last time you were here," the woman paused and rifled through the small amount of papers in Sarah's medical folder, "was when you stepped on that rusty nail at the beach club. My goodness. That was over two years ago. Don't you make time for a yearly physical?"

Sarah shook her head, the knot in her stomach tightened, her knees knocked together. "I don't seem to have time to keep up with all that. No offense, but I'd rather talk things over with Doc privately. I know you normally do a standard intake so he enters knowing what he's dealing with," Sarah replied. "This is a bit more complicated."

Shelby sent a weird look her way. No doubt the woman surmised something wasn't kosher. One of the reasons Sarah had a limited file at the Wellness Center was due in fact it was protocol she be checked out after each operation by CIA doctors as well as undergo a briefing with an Agency shrink before moving onto the next assignment…and when she wasn't feeling well. Sarah had broken with protocol. So be it.

Shelby, in the dark as to Sarah's "real" job, was one of the first friends she'd made on her return home four years ago. They were "best buddies" as Shelby called them, sharing dinner and drinks every couple of weeks. Sarah wished she could really share her true identity, but given the circumstances, Sarah happily settled for having one good friend to "girl-talk" with. A dreaded feeling crept over her that she might need Shelby more than ever in the months to come.

Shelby's personal history was the polar opposite of Sarah's, even though the two were the same age. Shelby's parents were both doctors; Sarah's had passed away years ago. The woman's parents invited her on a number of occasions to family gatherings at their massive estate nestled in the dunes in Southampton. Several times it was evident to Sarah how disappointed they were Shelby hadn't followed in their footsteps and gone to medical school. Her friend often bemoaned the fact her parents would never be happy with her decision to become a Physician's Assistant. As far as Shelby was concerned her parents would have to learn to live with her decision since she had no intention of moving on further in the medical profession. Shelby liked her life just the way it was and shared she was very happy not to be on call 24/7. Money was not high on her priority list. Shelby was content to own a small condo by the marina in Hampton Beach. She relished the fact her life wasn't complicated dealing with men who saw her as nothing more than a way to the prestige and status her rich parents could offer. She'd been burned one too many times.

Sarah didn't blame Shelby one bit. Since March, she'd had a taste of life in the 24/7 fast lane. In fact, she'd come to want nothing more to do with the life she'd been living.

Several days ago, after much reflection and deep reservation, she sent her letter of resignation, via certified mail, to Director Elizabeth Hallock. The woman would *not* be happy upon its receipt. Sarah dreaded the phone call and summons that would follow. There was little doubt she would be "invited" to the woman's private compound in D.C. Sarah was one of Elizabeth's best agents. The older woman would do everything in her power to change her mind. Sarah had nightmares of the day she'd have to explain the reasons behind her resignation in a face-to-face meeting. She was thankful her contract clearly stated she had the right to bow out at a certain point or when "circumstances presented a clear and present danger to the operative". Sarah could be given a desk job back in D.C., but that was not what she wanted. What she yearned for was a normal life like those around her.

"Hey, friend! Are you with me? Want to lie down? You're a bit pale."

Sarah snapped out of her reverie. Shelby had placed the data sheet in her file and was attempting to hand her a hospital gown. A wary look crossed her friend's face. "Take everything off, except your panties. Doc will be in momentarily."

Sarah took hold of the gown. "Did you bring him into work today?"

The Hamptons were known for their concierge doctors. Doc Davis was a legend in his own right as far as the townies were concerned. The man had a medical degree, won a multitude of service awards, but never had wanted to obtain a driver's license. It was twenty-five miles from Hampton Beach to the Wellness Center in Riverhead. The days he set aside to work in the clinic he set out at six in the morning and started the long walk. Somewhere along the way, a townie would be passing by and give him a lift the rest of the way, no matter if the clinic was out of the way from where the individual needed to go. Doc was loved and treasured by all. And, best of all, he made house calls. For free.

Shelby walked to the door of the examination room. "As a matter of fact, I did. I even brought him a latte. Remember how he sputtered the first time he tried 'that citified stuff'? No more. Wants me to bring him 'a cappuccino'. Told me he wants to 'broaden my horizons' before he's put in his grave." Shelby and Sarah burst out laughing at the same time. "Doc's a character. I love working for him." She motioned to the prep gown for Sarah to get dressed. "Fair warning. Doc's fitting you in. He's running late due to Tommy Rogers needing stitches. Can't imagine he'll be more than twenty minutes."

"Fine with me. I'm just grateful he could see me." *Then I can get Mrs. E. off my back. She's called every day since we talked. Does the woman ever let anything drop?* Sarah clutched the gown to her chest and breathed a sigh of relief when the door closed. The minute she heard her file being stuffed into the bin on the outside of the door, she hastily stripped off her clothes per Shelby's instructions and laid them on the nearby chair. With the gown open in the back, she hopped up onto the exam table. Her body shivered. Was she cold from the A/C or was she reacting to what she surmised what might be true. She said a silent pray it was the former.

As she waited, Sarah glanced around the room. Doc was into local art and photos of Hampton Beach and its surrounding areas. Most of the older buildings on Main Street had changed over time, but a talented artist, Liz Ayers, brought the past back to life in black and white etchings. A local photographer, Robert Seifert, captured Doc's love of the beach, especially the sunsets and sunrises at Jetty Four. Jetty Four was sacred to the townies. It's where everyone hung out when the summer people came to town.

Hearing Doc's booming voice in the hall, Sarah felt a bevy of butterflies in her stomach; her heart raced. If Shelby took her BP right then, the reading would be twenty points higher than when she'd taken it initially. It wasn't due to white coat syndrome, either. While waiting for Doc, Sarah mentally counted out the days since July 5th. Pulling the gown tight around her, she thought, not her. It couldn't be possible.

The door opened and Sarah found herself staring into a pair of sparkling blue eyes. Doc Davis was closing on seventy-five years young, as he liked to point out, and still going strong. Standing close to six-foot tall, his hair was as white as snow. He closed the door and for that brief moment when he studied her, she read the fatherly concern etched on his face.

Doc laid her paperwork on the counter, rolled his stool from the corner, stopped it front of her, and sat down. Pursing his lips, he spoke in a gentle tone. "Something's got to be really wrong if you've come to my office, Sarah Adams. What's up?" His hand patted her knee. "Lay your cards on the table and tell me what the trouble is. There's hardly anything on that intake paper. Remember what we discuss within these four walls stays between the two of us."

Tears welled up in her eyes. Oh, for Pete's sake! Not the water works again! She felt a wad of tissues pressed into the palm of her hand.

"It's my body, Doc. Something's really off kilter. Granted, since March, I've been pushing myself way too hard. A lot of stress." She watched as the doctor's right eyebrow arched. Was he shocked, surprised, or did he know? She would share what she could. Sarah began to tick off the items on her list. "I'm not eating. No appetite. I want to crawl into bed and not wake up for a week. No, make that a month. To be honest, I feel like I did when I had mono in college, but I don't have a sore throat or swollen glands. My boobs hurt. I'm totally drained, can't stay focused. It's a chore to get out of bed in the morning.

"I usually run seven to ten miles every other day as part of my exercise routine. Now," she locked her eyes on his and sighed in disgust, "I can barely put one foot in front of the other. Between the fifteen hours a day at the beach club and visiting Gram and Pop every day at assisted living, I'm burning the candle at both ends. Am I making any sense?" Doc didn't reply. He just sat silent, studying her. "I haven't had any time for myself in four years. When I was a kid, I used to have to get B-12…"

"Stop right there." He put his hand up, palm facing her, before she could say another word. "Boy, it sure is a good thing you came in. Let's take one thing at a time, shall we? I knew there was a problem the minute I saw those bags under your eyes. I can see them even under your tan."

More tears trickled down her cheeks. "And…this! This crying! This is not me. I. Don't. Cry." She blew her nose into the wad of tissues.

"Hush, now. Take big, deep breaths. We're going to figure this out." Doc rose from his stool and patted her on the shoulder, his voice filled with compassion. "Now it's my job to see what's turned you upside down and inside out. You're absolutely right in reading your body signals."

Doc spent the next thirty minutes probing and checking her out. When he finished, he sat back down, and placed his hand on her knee, giving it a reassuring squeeze. "I think I can safely say we can easily get to the bottom of what's going on. How's that sound?"

Sarah was happy to hear his proclamation, letting out a huge sigh of relief. She made an attempt to smile. "I feel as if the weight of the world might be lifting off my shoulders, Doc."

"Before I make any pronouncements, I'm going to draw blood. It will take about a week for the results to come back. I'm going to have Shelby do a full panel."

Her head snapped up. "A full panel? That sounds serious."

Doc Davis got up and went to the counter to write the script for her blood draw. "Sarah, it's nothing to worry about. It's SOP. Standard Operating Procedure."

Sarah's brow furrowed. "What are you checking for?" Her knuckles turned white as she squeezed the table.

"Nothing serious. I do think it would be a good idea to test your hormone levels. You're thirty-two. Sometimes perimenopause can present symptoms even at your age."

"Menopause? What?" She practically shrieked as the dreaded "M" word worked through her brain. "But...How can..." The man chuckled at her expense. "Why are you laughing?"

"Sarah!" Doc came and stood in front of her, his right hand grabbing a hold of her chin. "Look at me. Peri-menopause can start to do weird things to women's bodies, especially when there's stress. Am I making sense?"

Sarah hesitated. Oh, how she wanted to tell him everything. "Yes."

"Want to tell me what's going on?"

"Only what I told you. There are a few things I can't talk about right now."

The doctor shot a quizzical look her way and went on as if he was satisfied with her answers. She could tell by the expression on his face he didn't buy into everything she said. "The panel will make sure your hormones and insides are operating within the proper range. If not, I'll know what to do to get you back on track. It may simply be a lack of certain vitamins and your diet. You've dropped a few pounds." He paused, looked her in the eye, and cleared his throat. "By any chance are you nauseous?"

She emphatically answered, "No." She hated to lie, but there was only so much she could deal with.

"When was the last time you had your period?"

Not surprised by his question, she sat mute.

Fingers snapped in front of her face. When she looked at him, Doc had cocked his head at a strange angle, looking a bit more inquisitive than before. "That should be a fairly easy question to answer."

She shrugged her shoulders. "Not for me it isn't. I've always been irregular. In high school, I worked out rigorously with the gymnastics team. My period all but disappeared. The doctor told me that was normal from over exercising. Gram told me not to worry. Since I've been home, it's been hit or miss. Sorry I can't be more forthcoming."

Doc walked to the counter and jotted down a few more notes. "You'd be surprised that that happens to a lot of women. What about your sex life? Are you on the pill?"

Her face reddened hearing the kind, gentle man asking her about such an intimate detail in her life. She stared up at the white ceiling, not wanting to face him. She crossed her fingers. "Non-existent. And no, I'm not on the pill. Don't have a need to be."

Doc seemed to mumble something under his breath and swiveled back around to look at her. This time he wore a broad smile on his face, her folder in his hand. "Well, I'm done for now. Shelby will call as soon as the results are in. We'll get together. How's that sound?"

"Good. I'll relax when I know when things are definitive. Any advice in the meantime?"

"Try to make a routine to your day. Get a bit of exercise. Your body is telling you that you need rest. Take a short nap… every day. I know your schedule is difficult, but try. Better yet, how about a vacation? Since you don't have much of an appetite, try your best to eat three healthy meals or six small meals a day. You *have* to eat. Now, get your clothes on. I'll send

Shelby in to draw that blood. Tell Matt I said to ease up a bit on the job hours. I can give you a script that states that if you want."

Sarah shook her head vehemently. "No. I get comp time. Thanks, Doc." *The last thing I need is for Matt or anybody else knowing I've been to see the town doctor.*

Thirty minutes later, Sarah was on her car's phone informing her assistant at the beach club she was on her way back from her "errand". As she drove over Jessup Bridge, the Sunfish came into view. Parking her new car in her assigned slot, her entire body gave in to all the pent-up feelings she experienced at the Wellness Center. Her body shook, tears ran down her cheeks, her body wracked with sobs. *Inhale. Exhale. Try to relax. It's over. You did it. You didn't have a choice.* She had a suspicion Doc had known exactly what the tests would show, but played his part to keep her calm and steady. Now it was up to her to decide what to do once the results were in. Life, if she'd read her body signals right, was about to change dramatically.

She thought back to that morning waking up beside Rick. Her instincts as an agent took over seeing him in such a deep sleep. Sneaking out of bed, she looked for the "evidence" as she threw on her blue gown. Tip-toeing around to his side of the bed, she found what she was looking for. Using a tissue, she picked them up and stuffed them in her evening bag. She felt like a member of a CSU team, cleaning up after a crime. After writing the note, she silently left the cottage wishing things could be different. Knowing there was an old Jeep hidden behind the barn with its keys in the ignition, she decided to borrow it. Once on the road, headed for her apartment, she kept one eye on the road and reached for her purse.

Looking inside, she spied what she'd taken. How could this happen and to her of all people? And there wasn't one person in all of Hampton Beach she could tell, not even Shelby... that during her passionate encounter with the man of her dreams, she was sure one of the condoms broke.

CHAPTER FIVE

September 26th

Earlier in the day, after another tense morning standoff with Matt, Sarah called Shelby. She couldn't wait until the weekend for their planned "girl-talk" night out. A typical evening was dinner at Magic's Pub, followed by binge watching their favorite streaming TV shows at each other's apartment. Pajamas were a must as well as several bottles of Merlot or Chardonnay for good measure. The two would briefly argue over which show to watch. The reality of drinking three to four glasses of wine and attempting to drive home sober had led to the PJ parties. The last thing either needed was a DUI ticket on her spotless driving record.

It took a while to connect with Shelby since it was a work day. The clinic, from Sarah's observation, was a non-stop turnstile of patients. Her friend was normally exhausted at the end of a shift. However, when Shelby answered with a cheery

"What's up?" silence followed Sarah's request for Shelby to move their Saturday night get-together to that night.

Finally, Shelby replied, "Listen. I can't do dinner. How about I come over around seven? We'll do TV, wine and PJs. I'll bring a change of scrubs since I just found out I have to sub in on the early shift tomorrow."

"Great. Can't wait to see you." Sarah tried her best to camouflage her tone, hoping to come across enthusiastic. Now as she straightened up her living room, Sarah wondered if it had been a good idea to call and invite her dear friend over. Could she stay calm and not let go of all the stress welling up inside? Was she going to be able make it through the night and not tell her best friend the real truth about what had happened between her and Rick?

Dressed in her PJs, grey sweats and a very baggy George Washington tee shirt, Sarah straightened up the last of the magazines strewn on the floor into a neat and tidy pile. She placed them on the side table next to her sofa. Opening its drawer, she took out two coasters covered with starfish designs and placed them on the antique footlocker she used as a coffee table. She'd left work two hours early, getting the evil eye from her boss. The few extra hours gave Sarah more time to take a leisurely shower and make a list of the final things Matt wanted to accomplish at the beach club the next day. She even had time to down a bowl of chicken noodle soup with saltine crackers on the side. She was doing as Doc instructed. Her appetite had slowly returned. Eyeing the single wine glass on the counter, she was glad at least her best friend would be able to truly relax tonight. She, on the other hand, would be drinking iced water or ginger ale, more likely the former.

Noting the living room was ready to receive company, she strolled into the galley kitchen mulling over the last ten days.

Doc Davis called her to come to his private office on Main Street, confirming her worst nightmare. She was surprised how well she handled the news, half expecting the waterworks to spew. It took only minutes for him to go over her test results, ever the consummate professional, although she spied him glancing at her strangely from time to time. After words of advice and options, he gave her the name of an OB/GYN doctor to see from that point forward. The woman doctor came highly recommended and could be "trusted with your secret". As she walked out of the office complex and got into her car she pondered if he was alluding to the fact she was pregnant or that he knew Rick was the father of her child. Doc had also been invited to the wedding and reception. Did he see and think the same as Mrs. E? No. No way. Even if he did, he would certainly keep it to himself.

When Doc gave her the advice to take a long vacation, she chuckled inwardly when she heard him mutter under his breath, "If *she'll* let you." Sarah recalled the events from two years earlier. Doc became involved in the aftermath care of Megan, Matt's wife. Megan nearly drowned during her CIA mission on Block Island and there'd been the possibility she was exposed to a hazardous toxin. Not having an Agency doctor nearby, the Director broke protocol, enlisting Doc's help, deputizing him on the spot. He'd become an official agent of the CIA. Had he since relinquished his duties? Should her biggest worry be that her predicament be shared before she'd a chance to privately talk with the Director?

Several days after her visit to see Doc, Sarah cornered Matt in his office at the beach club. What had started as a bright, sunny day had turned into a day from hell. When asked if she could take a month's vacation from her duties, he looked at her as if she had four heads.

"Are you kidding me?" Matt's face reddened not from sunburn, but from anger. She was stunned. The man standing across from her on the opposite of the desk wasn't the man she was used to dealing with. "I can't part with you now. You do remember we're in the process of closing up for the winter? What the hell are you thinking? Absolutely not!"

Just in case she received a negative response to her request, Sarah came prepared, armed with ammunition. Standing in front of him, she ticked off her list on her fingers. One, the fact she'd only eight days off in the last eleven years. Two, she needed time to spend time with her grandparents to work with the facility on a new medical plan for her grandfather. And finally, her need to "get-away". That point hit home big time when she noted he and Megan took a month for an extended honeymoon to Greece and its islands because Megan had "needed a break". From the look on his face, Matt was indeed shocked she'd taken him on in such a fashion. But he finally caved. They called a truce, putting their heads together to find a happy medium that worked for both parties. It was decided if she could stay until the twenty-seventh, which was tomorrow, leaving him a final list of "to-dos" for the remaining employees, she could go and take her "break" or "whatever the hell you plan on doing".

Matt would never know, nor was she going to share with anyone else, her intended plan – to leave Hampton Beach.

Sarah recalled the look of suspicion he gave her when she said good-bye. After all, he, too, married a spy.

Out of the blue, Sarah felt the urge to let go of her frustration and emotions. "Damn! You are pregnant, girl!" Saying it out loud made the reality sink in. Reaching inside the cupboard next to the sink for a tall glass to fill with water, she raised her voice. "So, Sarah Ann, what would Gram tell you to do?"

"Do about what?"

Startled, Sarah let go of the glass watching it fly through the air. She caught hold of it just as it came within inches of crashing onto the kitchen counter. "Shelby! What-what…"

Shelby stood in the middle of her living room carrying one very large bottle of wine and a bag of cookies and treats, no doubt from her favorite pastry shop. A large, red tote bag lay at her feet, her blanket, pajamas and clothes for the next day sticking out from within. Her favorite pillow stuffed into a Wonder Woman pillowcase was on the floor.

"I repeat," Shelby stated. "*What* is Gram going to tell you to do? When you called to get together on a work night, I told myself something was amiss. I'm right. Aren't I?"

Just like Mrs. E., Shelby read her like a book.

Leaving the glass on the counter, Sarah walked from where she stood and came to the aid of her friend. "No. It's been a rough couple of days at work. Here, let me take something." Suddenly it dawned on her Shelby was standing in her apartment, not pounding on the front door. "Hey! How'd you get in?"

"I rang that damn doorbell ten times, girlfriend. Almost thought of dialing 911 until I remembered you said that fake hedgehog out there," she jerked her head towards the door, "was a key-keeper. Which, by the way, is really weird since you always so hyper about security."

Sarah walked to the open front door and closed it. "I can't believe I didn't hear you."

"Because you were talking – TO – YOURSELF!" Shelby eyed her curiously and stepped over her tote bag and pillow. She made her way around Sarah and walked into the narrow kitchen. "This wine needs to chill. I swear I was out on your porch for fifteen minutes." Shelby opened the refrigerator and placed the wine on the shelf, closing the door with her hip. "So, again. You were talking to yourself. Care to share?"

Sarah wondered how much Shelby heard. "Yes, I was talking to myself. Matt needs a list for the club tomorrow. I was just musing out loud."

Shelby questioningly peered at her through black eyeglasses. "Uh, if that's the story you're going with, I'm going to change. Then, you're going to answer the real question you were asking yourself. For the record, I've got a few of my own. As a matter of fact, there's a small list."

She brushed past Sarah, making her way down the hallway towards the guest bedroom. Sarah thought then perhaps tonight might not have been a good idea. *As an agent you know not to break with a pattern someone is familiar with. You should have kept Saturday's dinner date. What were you thinking? You've unleashed the beast. Shelby will be relentless.*

While Shelby changed, Sarah busied herself setting up the sofa for their night of entertainment. She pulled her Sherpa blanket from the club chair and draped it over her designated end of the sofa. Circling the coffee table, she bent over and picked up Shelby's pillow from the floor and placed it on the other end of the blue-checked couch. Sarah's mouth broke out into a wide grin knowing her best friend would be out soon carrying her favorite cartoon character blanket of the day. Having to deal with so many children at Doc's clinic, the woman took her job to the extreme even when it came to her personal life. That was what Sarah loved about Shelby. She was true to herself and her values. And she was plain fun to be around.

"There." Shelby reentered the living room, dressed in PJs. "Let me grab us some wine. You can answer a few questions, then we'll crank up a show." Shelby marched into the kitchen, opening the drawer where the corkscrew was located.

"Ah, Shel..."

"Yeah?" Pop! The bottle opened, followed by silence. "Uh... Sarah? Why is there only one wine glass on your counter? Did you break the other one?"

Sarah cringed, not wanting to reply.

"Sarah?" The question was asked again.

Sarah felt Shelby's eyes on her, but she didn't have the courage to turn and face her friend. What plausible reason could she give?

"I guess I know what to get you for Christmas, huh?" There was a hint of laughter in Shelby's voice. Sarah had a feeling her friend was trying to make light of what might be a night of serious discussion. Sarah knew Shelby and vice versa.

Feeling on edge, Sarah replied, trying her best to keep her voice steady and calm. *Pray that Shelby doesn't know.* "Listen. I'm passing on the alcohol tonight. There's a glass on the counter. Can you fill it with ice water?"

The normal flow of conversation that usually occurred suddenly ceased. The silence in the kitchen was deafening. Sarah only heard the sound of liquids being poured into glasses. Finally, footsteps approached, and Sarah felt the cushion give way on her right side. A glass of water was placed in front of her on the coffee table.

You can do this. Drawing in a deep breath, Sarah turned, pasted on her best smile and asked, "So, what should we watch tonight? How about one of those British detective mysteries?" She prayed she sounded nonchalant.

Shelby was about to settle into her side of the couch when she stopped. "Sounds good. Press start, girlfriend." Pointing to the remote, she said, "I'll be right back. I forgot the munchies."

* * *

"Hey!... Sleepyhead!... Wake up!"

Sarah felt a hand nudging her in the ribcage. Her brain foggy from sleep, she realized she had drifted off during the show, slumping onto the arm of the sofa. Bolting upright, she apologized, "Oh my gosh. I can't believe I dozed off like that." She reached for some popcorn in the bowl on the table trying her best to pretend nothing happened. "Fill me in, Shel. What did I miss? The body was at the foot of the basement steps..."

Shelby took the TV remote from the coffee table and clicked off the television. Her attention was fully on Sarah, her eyes assessing her up and down. She reached over and touched her hand to Sarah's forehead. "You're not running a temperature and you don't seem sick. Honestly, I've been worried since Doc gave strict orders your tests go right onto his desk. *Immediately.* Out with it."

Inwardly, Sarah breathed a sigh of relief. "Shelby, there are some things…"

"No. Don't go there. We're best friends. Right? You know things about me no one else does. I've always leveled with you, no matter what. If there's something…" she hesitated briefly, "wrong, you know I'm here for you."

It was the moving tribute of friendship and having Shelby move beside her and place her arm around her shoulder in a loving gesture that made Sarah cave into the stress she'd been experiencing. The waterworks started with tears pouring down her cheeks. All Sarah could do was nestle into the comfort her friend's shoulder provided and cry her heart out.

Shelby held her tight. "Take big deep breaths. Let it all out. Here." Sarah took the glass of water Shelby offered into her shaking hands. "Take a sip and tell me why you're taking a month's vacation from the beach club?"

Her tears and sobs had drowned out Shelby's soothing words of comfort, but *that* question snapped Sarah from her pity party. "How did you know about that?"

"When I was at the bakery picking up my munchies, Matt and Megan were huddled together at the table by the door. I heard him tell her how upset he is tomorrow is your last day at the club. He doesn't know what he's going to do without you. Sarah, that guy doesn't get rattled very often, but he really was upset. Megan had all she could do to calm him down." Shelby paused, then, in a soft voice asked, "Did you just up and quit?"

Sighing, Sarah shook her head and replied, "No, I didn't. I need some time off. Matt's really mad I want to do it now on such short notice. I'm exhausted, Shelby. It's affecting my health. That's why I came in to see Doc. My body's never felt like this. Ever."

Leaning back into her corner of the couch with some space between them, Shelby eyed Sarah and pronounced, "That would explain everything."

"What exactly do you mean by that?"

"Slap me if I'm going over the line here. But, *you*, my friend, are pregnant with Rick Stockton's baby. It's not going to be long before people around here figure it out. You forget almost the whole town was at the wedding."

The wedding. The wedding. The wedding. Those words echoed over and over through Sarah's mind. Suddenly she felt flushed and overheated. Sweat broke out on her brow. Standing up, thinking it might help if she got her blood circulating, she became nauseous and thought her supper wasn't going to stay down. The room started to spin.

"Shelby, I think I need… " Sarah cried out.

The last thing she recalled as she went down for the count was the look of shock on her friend's face. Blackness claimed her as she crumpled into a heap onto her living room floor.

CHAPTER SIX

September 30th

Late. Late. Late. A stickler for punctuality, Sarah was growing more upset as the clock ticked away. As she tried on the dress she'd picked out to wear to the baptism, she spied herself in the bedroom mirror and was horrified how it hugged her belly a bit too tight. The small baby bump was noticeable. Add to that she felt as if her boobs were crushed into the bodice of the red and black striped dress.

"That one's not going to work. I hope you kept the receipt." Shelby arrived earlier with an armful of dresses after a panicked phone call from Sarah. "Here. This one's looser on top and, besides, it's high-waisted. That should help hide you know what." Shelby threw the navy-blue dress at her. "I think it's going to be the best choice out of the bunch. You know after our talk, I was going to ask you whether or not you'd picked out some clothes to fit since you're adamant about hiding this pregnancy. It's probably the last thing on your list, but you better have a clothes plan. Sweatpants and sweatshirts aren't going to cut it forever."

While Shelby talked, Sarah tried on the blue dress.

Shelby's coming to her aid and her constant talking, since she'd walked in the front door, was a relief since Sarah really didn't feel much like participating in any sort of conversation.

Her friend continued, "I'm glad you confided in me about Rick. However, hiding the fact you're pregnant, especially in this town, is going to require some serious thinking and planning. Two heads are going to be better than one, if you catch my drift."

Sarah nodded in agreement. However, she was in a hurry to be elsewhere. "I can't get into that right now. I have to get to St. Mark's." *And I'm not about to tell you I have every intention of leaving within the next few weeks.*

"After all I've done for the Hallock clan, I cannot believe I didn't get an invite." Sarah glanced over to where her friend sat on the bed. Clearly there was a hurt tone in Shelby's voice. "Mrs. E. got one as did Doc. Hell. What am I? Chopped liver? I could have been your buffer against you know who."

Sarah glanced into the long white mirror hanging on the back of her bedroom door. Oh, much, much better, she thought, twirling about. She wished she could give Shelby her invitation to attend the baptism now the truth about the pregnancy had been confirmed. However, Sarah had promised to go, and if she didn't show, Mrs. E. and the Hallocks would never forgive her. Looking back at her friend she didn't know quite what to say. Shelby was obviously hurt by not getting invited. She attempted to find some excuse to appease her best friend. "From what I've heard, Kate and John were adamant about 'family' being front and center. Whatever that means. Can you come and zip me up?"

Shelby rose, walked over, and did as requested. Seeing Shelby's smile of approval made Sarah's confidence grow. She could do this. Then, the thought of what she was about to do about her situation hit her squarely in the middle of her forehead. Was she doing the right thing by leaving Hampton Beach? Would she be okay without her best friend by her side, especially when the baby came? She pushed those thoughts to the back of her brain and concentrated on the task at hand. Sarah slipped on her flats, grabbed her purse, and headed for the door.

"Wait!" Shelby called out.

"What is it? I've got to go. You know how to lock up."

"It's cold outside. The sea breeze has really whipped up. Take this shawl and drape it over and around you for warmth." Shelby came over and, like a fashion designer fitting her model, draped the blue-flowered shawl over and around Sarah's shoulders. "There. You'll be warm. Besides, the shawl will give extra coverage where you need it." Her friend winked at her. "If you know what I mean."

Sarah smiled in return, understanding, and gave her friend a hug. "What would I do without you?"

Shelby shrugged her shoulders. "Some day I have a feeling I'm going to need your help. Now, go. I wish I could be there to see Rick's face when you tell him."

Sarah stopped dead in her tracks, closing the door she'd just opened. She turned around and looked her friend squarely in the eyes. "Shelby, I have no intention of telling Rick. I'm going to raise this baby on my own. There are things I can't tell you. Please just respect my decision… for now."

Sarah watched Shelby's jaw sag in disbelief. "You can't… I mean…God, Sarah. Now you're acting and sounding as if you're one of the Hallocks when they worked for the CIA. What are you planning? To go undercover somewhere?"

Sarah shot her friend a telling look, opened the door and closed it behind her. She would never forget the look of shock as it dawned on Shelby what Sarah implied. But rest assured her secret was safe. Best friends didn't desert each other in their hour of need.

* * *

St. Mark's Church
40 Main Street
Hampton Beach, Long Island

Within minutes, Sarah pulled into the church's parking lot. Shit! People had parked everywhere. There wasn't a space to be found. Seeing a spot on the newly mowed lawn, she decided she would deal with the wrath of the good reverend later. At that moment, she was late and had to be inside and in her seat. She was cutting it close.

After locking her car, she sprinted up the granite steps and through the pillars to the church entrance. Heaving open the heavy front door, a sudden gust of wind almost made her lose her grip on its large gold handle. She prayed she could quietly slide into a back pew.

However, once inside, she was taken aback as she peered through the windows of the narthex doors leading into the nave of the church. All the seats from the front of the church to the back row were taken. Damn!

As her eyes roamed the venue, she laid eyes on Reverend Wade. He was upfront by the baptismal font instructing Matthew and Megan Hallock, John Jr.'s godparents, as well as Kate, the baby's mother, with her husband, John Clinton. Final directions were underway. From experience, Sarah knew only too well how thorough the good reverend was for Episcopalian pomp and circumstance.

"Excuse me, ma'am." Sarah turned around to find Tom, one of the club's employees, dressed in a black suit. He was holding out a program. "Here. Take this. The ceremony is about to start so you better find a seat. I think there might be a few places up front on the right by the pulpit." Tom opened the door and motioned for her to step inside.

With program in hand, she drew in a deep breath. "Well then, I better get a move on." Giving Tom a thankful smile, she said, "I certainly don't want to miss this." Sarah stepped through the open doorway scanning the mass of people. Many women wore hats on their heads virtually blocking her view of possible places to sit.

To Sarah it seemed as if everyone turned upon hearing the squeak of the large wooden doors. Eyes fell upon her when she made her entrance.

As she glanced down the long, red-carpeted center aisle to the right side of the church by the pulpit, suddenly, from out of nowhere, a hand shot up four rows from where Tom indicated there might be a seat. The hand was attached to a lace handkerchief. Its owner was attempting to get Sarah's attention. When she spied Mrs. E., she was relieved. Because of the multitude of things on her mind lately, coupled with the reality of facing Rick, she'd completely forgotten the woman told her she'd save her a seat.

Making sure her shawl was securely wrapped in strategic places, she strolled down the aisle, her head held high. She nodded to a few members of the Hallock family sitting in the first few pews close to the baptismal font. Arriving at the fourth pew, she bowed her head towards the altar and slid in beside Mrs. E. Being so close to the front only reminded her of the day of Courtney's wedding. She'd been surprised Helen had thought so much of her to sit her in the family section. She had a perfect vantage point to view Rick, and he her.

"Finally. You made it. Where have you been?" Mrs. E. whispered, squeezing Sarah's knee. "I was beginning to think you weren't going to show." She stopped, a perplexed look on her face. "Where's that beautiful dress we went shopping for? Whatever possessed you to put on that old thing?"

Trying to get the woman to lower her voice, Sarah whispered her reply. "I took the one I bought back to the store. It just didn't fit right." *I'm not lying. It didn't. Only she doesn't need to know why.* She continued, "I almost did back out. I'm so nervous about seeing Rick, if you really must know. I don't know what I was thinking when I said 'yes' to this."

Trying not to look conspicuous, she pivoted her head to the left and right, then glanced over her shoulder at the crowd behind her. Sarah tried her best to zero on the man in question, but he seemed to be MIA. *Maybe it's better this way. Go off and do things on your terms like you told Shelby.*

"Rick's not here yet." Mrs. E. leaned over and spoke quietly into her right ear. "But he will be. Rumor has it he had to fly from New York this morning." An odd look passed over her face as she once again took in Sarah's apparel. "What's with the shawl? You look like a little old lady all bundled up for winter. Take that off. It's hot in here."

The woman started to tug at the shawl, but Sarah covered Mrs. E.'s hand with her own. "Listen, I was late due to a phone call from the assisted living." She crossed her fingers as she told yet another little white lie. Lightning should have struck her dead being she was in church. "It took me forever to get the zipper up on the dress and when I got here there was nowhere to park. Besides, I'm cold. I grabbed the first thing I could find when I ran out the door."

"Well, considering everything, you look lovely. Even if you're not wearing that beautiful dress from the boutique." The woman seemed a bit miffed, but Sarah knew she was joking. It was then Mrs. E. reached for Sarah's chin and grabbed hold of it. Turning her face from side to side, the woman erupted with glee. "You're wearing makeup! And you even had your hair done…with highlights."

Shelby had worked her magic on her hair after dragging her to Macys in Hampton Bays earlier in the morning. Her best friend insisted on paying for her face to be professionally made-up by a friend at the Clinique counter. As far as Sarah was concerned, it was a bit of overkill. Her friend was bound and determined Sarah look her best if Rick was going to be at the baptism.

Sarah raised her fingers to her lips to silence the woman beside her. Glancing down at the program in her lap, she brushed away an imaginary piece of lint. "You don't need to tell the whole town."

"I, for one, think she looks stunning." A deep, masculine voice rang out from over her shoulder.

Rick Stockton was back in town.

CHAPTER SEVEN

Rick braced himself for the steely glare he expected to receive from the eyes of the woman sitting in the pew. He'd come to get answers from her and explain how the night they spent together was unlike any other in his book. As he stood in the aisle, Sarah never acknowledged his presence. Oh, she knew he was there. Her body had stiffened upon hearing him mention how beautiful she looked. Leave it to Mrs. Eckart to be the one happy to see him. Her grin was a mile wide. At least some one was in his corner.

Deciding he was on shaky ground, he thought it better to take the high road. Rick politely asked, "Is this seat taken? I can manage to squeeze in beside the two of you. My plane was late touching down at Gabreski due to the winds. The pilot wanted to turn around when we went wings up. I told Jake if he coveted his job, he'd better land my plane…in Hampton Beach."

Mrs. Eckart subtly slid a tiny bit farther to her right, nudging Sarah to do the same. Sarah turned to the older woman, muttering something under her breath Rick couldn't quite catch. Did Mrs. Eckart know what transpired between them? No. Sarah coveted her privacy. She'd never divulge such an intimate detail. Rick wished he'd taken more of an opportunity to get to know more of the residents of the area when he'd come to town in March. He'd been there to clean up the mess with Thomas's embezzlement problem having little time to interact with people unrelated to Operation Hallock Farm. Perhaps it was time to line up people who'd want to see Sarah have her happily ever after.

Again, he made a plea to take a seat. "Sarah, would you mind? There's really no other place to sit. I think I can squeeze my large frame in the space beside you."

It was then the woman of his dreams looked up. He cringed inwardly seeing her dagger-like stare. "By all means, take a seat. We'll make room." From her tone, she sounded disgusted he was there. Well, he had news for her. He wasn't leaving Hampton Beach until he'd the chance to smooth things over. Even though he was certain she was deliberately trying to make him believe she hated him, her note had been written with inferred passion. Finally beside her, he settled into the red cushioned seat letting his thoughts recall the night they shared; those that were totally inappropriate for church.

"So, how've you both been?" Rick casually asked. "Can I take your shawl, Sarah? Aren't you warm? I can put it..."

"I'm fine." He was taken aback by the terse tone in her voice.

Rick watched as she pulled the garment around her. "I just thought..." He stopped speaking. There was no way he was going to accomplish his mission in such a public arena. The two needed privacy.

"May I have your attention?" Reverend Wade's voice rang out through the church sound system. "It's time we get this baptism under way and welcome John Clinton, Jr. into God's family. Will the family take their appropriate places around the font."

Rick suddenly realized the church was deathly silent and the pastor stared directly in his direction.

"I do believe he's giving you the evil eye to shut up and be quiet." When he turned to look at Sarah, he spied a sly grin on her face.

He'd never known what to expect from her from one day to the next when they'd worked together. Sarah Adams had spunk, sass, a knock out body, and a natural beauty. Looking at her now, knowing three months had gone by, she seemed different somehow - a special glow radiated from her. He'd never met a woman like her. *Ever.* As far as he was concerned, there never would be another woman in his life... if things went according to plan.

With the ceremony starting, he moved closer to her. She tried to scoot away, a "do not touch me look" firmly spelled out on her face. Mrs. Eckart blocked her movement. Bless the woman.

"I just wanted to ask if you wouldn't mind sharing your program. I came in a different door and didn't get one. I'm not familiar with how all this works."

Sarah put her finger to her lips and promptly handed him the printed paper. "Here. Take it." She acted as if the program was a hot potato, quickly placing it in his hands. "I know the words by heart."

"You do?" Rick was truly surprised to know Sarah's faith played a part of who she was. Especially given the life she led within the Agency.

Sarah hissed, "Yes. Now be quiet."

Rick turned his head hoping to look down into the dark bedroom eyes he remembered. Instead, he found her staring intently towards the font and the ceremony's participants. Suddenly, everybody stood.

There was a rough tug on his coat sleeve.

"Pay attention. Stand up. Reverend Wade's going to name the baby." Sarah was clearly irritated.

Best to handle the woman beside him with kid gloves. She perturbed about something. "Walk me through this. I've never been to a baptism." He moved closer and pointed to the pamphlet. For the first time, she didn't cringe or move away.

"Megan is holding John Jr. and Matt is beside her. They're the godparents."

"Why?" Rick was surprised how truly interested in the Christian ritual he was. A vision of he and Sarah watching their own child, from the same spot where Kate and John stood, flashed through his mind.

"Godparents are the church's version of parents. If something should happen to the parents, godparents affirm the child will be brought up as Matt and Megan would want in the eyes of the church and its teachings."

Rick's eyes became glued to the sight of the pastor cradling the baby in the crook of his left arm. He dipped his right hand into the holy water from the font, making the sign of the cross on the baby's forehead. "In the name of the Father, the Son and the Holy Ghost, I baptize you, John Christopher Clinton, Jr. Amen."

"Amen." The congregation said in unison.

Turning to say something to Sarah, he stopped. She was using a tissue to dab away a tear, obviously moved by the ceremony. Realizing the ceremony had concluded, he gazed at the Hallock clan. Everyone hugged each other, passing the baby from one to the other. Rick was surprised he was actually jealous of all the love being displayed publicly by the gregarious family. The thought that this rite of passage hadn't happened yet to him weighed heavily on his mind. If life had played out as planned by this point in time, he'd have had a career, a beautiful home, and a family to complete his life. Instead, he'd become a workaholic. He desperately wanted the woman beside him to change all that.

Once again, the lady by his side captured his full attention. The fact she went from ignoring him on arrival, to sharing with him the meaning to each point of the service gave him hope all might not be lost.

"Rick? Are you headed to the country club for the reception?" Mrs. Eckart's question snapped him from his musings.

"Yes, of course. I'm here for the night given the weather. Thomas and Courtney graciously offered me a room at the main estate." He cleared his throat, giving the older woman a wink over Sarah's shoulder. Scanning the church, he saw it was empty except for the three of them. *Just as planned.* "I am going to need a ride though."

Mrs. Eckart picked up her coat and rapidly made for the other end of the pew. She called over her shoulder, "I have to run and pick up a few members of my family who had to close up the Luncheonette. Looks like it falls on Sarah to give you a lift to the country club."

"Touché. Nicely played." Sarah murmured sarcastically under her breath, but loud enough for him to hear.

"Listen, I just need a ride. Besides, we need to talk about that note." Sarah squeezed by him and began to march down the aisle to the front door. With long strides he finally caught up. *Break the ice. Get off the topic. For now.* "I honestly think this was all planned by the match making trio, if you want my opinion."

"I don't." She glanced up at him, a wary look in her eyes. "I'll give you a ride, but you, mister, are *not* driving. My car is brand new. The last time you insisted you *had* to drive, we landed in a ditch. My car, my rules."

He opened the narthex door and she passed through. "Understood. Let's get to the reception. We'll talk later."

"There will be no later." Her voice echoed in the small chamber.

Once outside, Rick followed Sarah to the church parking lot. His eyes opened wide spotting the lone car that remained. A Jaguar XE Portfolio. Say what? His lady had moved up in the world. What else was new in her life?

He barely had buckled his seat belt when the car shot out of from its parking space. The Jag sped out onto Main Street going from what seemed like zero to one hundred miles per hour in a split second. His head snapped back against the head rest. Out of the corner of his eye, he saw a triumphant look on Sarah's face.

Oh yes, he thought. Going on a lifetime ride with Sarah was definitely going to be an adventure. Rick immediately thought of the ring tucked away in his duffle bag in the trunk of Tom's car. There wasn't a doubt in his mind that his life was taking a turn in the right direction.

CHAPTER EIGHT

Hampton Beach Country Club

Sarah was quite pleased with herself. When she pulled out of the driveway of the church, she had intended to drive right to the country club, which was located across the street from the church. Instead, she made an instantaneous decision. Since she and Rick were already running slightly behind, she'd give him her version of a "quick" tour of the main drag of downtown in her new car. After all, hadn't he done the same thing to her four months earlier? Only that particular ride ended with her car being totaled.

From the stunned look she spied on his face when her new car hugged every turn, she hoped she was hitting home the point written in her note - things between them were over. O-V-E-R.

She'd concluded several weeks ago she wasn't going to give him a chance to get close even after replying in the affirmative to the RSVP. Now, with the dilemma she faced, could she pull it off? There was no way she intended to talk about the infamous night during any point at the reception. Sarah was content with the plans she'd made for her new life. Rick didn't work into any of them. When he'd said she was "stunning" back in the church, her heart almost did a complete one-eighty given her true feelings. Was she making a mistake? Should he know about the baby? *No way. That was so not going to happen.*

Back in March, during Operation Hallock Farm, she tried her best to dig up anything that would make her understand what made Rick tick. What was he really like on the inside" She came up short. Finally, she had to resort to dragging the information out of his sister, insisting the only way she and Rick could work well together was to know what he was like personally. It took three Saranac Summer Ales to loosen Courtney's tongue. Being a sister who clearly loved her sibling, she shared with Sarah her concern Rick chose to hop from one relationship to another. Courtney confided the man never had had a serious relationship in his entire adult life. She was convinced he was afraid to settle down. When pressed by Sarah for a reason why, Courtney said she believed he wasn't sure the woman he'd give his heart to would want him for himself alone, not his status and pocketbook. Courtney told Sarah she tried over and over to convince him there was a woman out there somewhere, but he'd given up, throwing himself into his work.

Pulling up to the entryway of the country club, Sarah taunted him. "Enjoy the ride?"

Rick moved the rearview mirror in his direction to adjust his tie. "You drove like that on purpose. We just had to..."

"Well, payback's a bitch." Pulling the shawl up and over her shoulders, she exited the car, handing her keys to the valet when the young man opened her door. She darted around the front of the car, not waiting for her unwanted companion. She couldn't climb the brick stairs of the clubhouse fast enough. Before she knew it, his hand was on her lower back. A jolt of electricity shot through her body.

"Back off, Rick." Thinking he'd do as she asked, he ignored her request and opened the French doors that led inside the fancy country club owned by Matt's brother, Ethan. She had no choice but to enter, issuing instructions as she moved forward. "Come with me. Over there."

"What about checking your coat?"

Sarah vehemently shook her head. "No time. There's the receiving line." She glanced up at the tall man beside her. Why, oh why, did he have to be so handsome? He made her want to throw her plans to the wind and see him the way she left him the morning after the wedding. Lowering her voice, she growled, "Please take your hand off my back! People will get the wrong idea."

Rick withdrew his hand, but he remained close at her side. He shook hands with each member of the family as they moved down the line. Arriving in front of Helen, Sarah prayed the woman wouldn't spew out, "Oh, how wonderful to see you together!" She wasn't in the mood to hear the matchmaker's clap-trap. All she could think of was how to get rid of the man trailing after her.

Helen's face brightened, a broad smile appeared. Her eyes lit up. "Rick! You made it. I hear you're staying at the main house this time." She took his hands in hers. "I'm so glad. It reminds me of the morning after the wedding when I found you…"

Rick, Sarah noted, quickly withdrew his hands from those of the Hallock matriarch. Was the man actually blushing? "I apologize Mrs. H. that we're a bit late." He shot her a telling look. "You'll have to excuse us. Sarah and I need to find where we're sitting. I promise we'll talk later. Ready, Sarah?"

Sarah, not wanting to cause a scene, politely responded, "It was a lovely celebration. The service was moving. You must be so happy to have another grandchild. But, Rick's right. We must find our seats." *For some reason I just know we're going to be together.*

Rick linked his arm through hers and pulled her away from the line. With her jaw clenched tight, she vowed she wouldn't make a scene. But, when she gazed up at him, she spied a smug look on his face. Oh, what she'd give to be able to slap it right off. But she was satisfied with her secret. He, and everyone else in the room, didn't know her bags were packed, her reservations made. Shelby was waiting to take her to the airport when she returned to her apartment.

Managing to release herself from his grasp, she walked to the round table holding the seating place cards. Odd. Both their names were missing.

A familiar voice rang out in the clamor around them. "Rick! Sarah!" The infamous handkerchief waved in the air three tables from where they presently stood. Having no choice, Sarah strode over to the table with Rick by her side. From the look on her face, Mrs. E. was delighted to see them both together. She gushed, "You're both sitting here with me and my family. Isn't that wonderful?"

Sarah pasted a smile on her face as she took her seat in the white wicker chair. *Isn't this what you wanted? Weren't you over the moon thinking Rick would be come? But all of that was before you found out you were pregnant with his child, wasn't it? You really thought it couldn't be true when you accepted the invitation.*

"Sarah? Sarah?" Fingers snapped in front of her eyes.

"Oh!" Apparently, Rick had asked her a direct question. "Sorry. What did you say?"

"I'm going to get a beer. What can I bring you? A martini? I know how you like them." His eyebrows wiggled playfully. Her thoughts flashed back to the wedding and the trouble over imbibing had caused.

Shaking her head vigorously, she replied, "No. I'm just going to drink the ice water."

"Really?" The man shot her a strange look. "There's top notch booze at the bar tonight."

Mrs. E. chimed in. "You always have a martini or a Cosmo. Did Doc give you meds and tell you not to drink?"

"Doc? Doc Davis?" Rick plopped down in the white chair beside her, taking hold of her right hand. Her leg started to shake under the table. She didn't like being under a microscope. But Rick was relentless with questions. "Are you sick? Why did you see Doc? What are you talking about, Mrs. Eckart?"

Sarah didn't want either Mrs. E. or Rick bringing attention to her, much less have anyone nearby hear about her visit to Doc's office. "Really, I'm just a bit run down. He put me on a strict vitamin regiment with a new diet plan to boost my energy levels and recommended I don't drink. Period. He said to think of it as if I was training for a marathon while my body rejuvenates itself." She turned to Rick and cocked her head towards the bar. "Better get your drink. Dinner's about to be served. The bar will probably close."

Again, Rick gave her a weird look, but rose from his chair, and walked away. Nope. She hadn't fooled him. The man hadn't believed a word of what she'd said. When Sarah glanced over her shoulder, her eyes landed on Thomas Hallock, standing at the bar, waving at Rick to come and talk. *Good. Now I'll just have Mrs. Busybody to deal with.*

In her left ear, she heard, "He doesn't believe you, and quite frankly, neither do I. You've always told me the truth. Look at me, Sarah Ann." When Sarah turned towards her dinner companion, she eyed Mrs. E. sitting with her arms crossed over her chest, her eyes locked on Sarah's. "May I remind you it was me who advised you to see Doc?" The woman wouldn't stop giving her the once over. "I must admit, though, you do look slightly better since the last time I saw you."

Sarah crossed her fingers over her heart. "Scout's honor. I'm really doing better."

"Baloney. You were never a Girl Scout."

Sarah counted to ten. She needed to nip this conversation in the bud if she was going to maintain her sanity. "Doc gave me a thorough check up. Even did a blood panel. It turns out my thyroid is working a bit slow, hence the fatigue. So...I have a ton of pills and instructions to get sleep, eat well and not drink."

"And that's why you're taking a month's vacation from the Sunfish?"

"You know about that? Matt promised me..."

"Matt promised you what?" Sarah stiffened hearing Rick's voice at her back. He'd returned to the table, sneaking up from behind.

Mrs. E., her eyes glued on Rick, stated, "Sarah's taking a *whole* month off from the Sunfish. Can you believe it? I can't." Mrs. E. shook her head in denial. The woman wasn't done. Sarah braced herself. "You *never* take time off. Did I not tell you at breakfast that job was why you were so exhausted?"

Back in his seat, Rick wouldn't let the topic drop either. Sarah couldn't catch a break. "Are you sure you're really going to be okay? If you're taking time off, why not come into the city? We'll take in some shows." Sarah's eyes widened at the very thought. "I have a separate apartment where you can rest and relax. We can..."

Sarah had had enough. "Stop. Please. Right now, I have priorities other than the beach club. First, myself. Second, I need to deal with my grandparents' financial situation. And to be quite honest, I just want time to veg."

A waitress placed a garden salad on the table in front of her. "Ma'am, I was asked to give you this." The waitress handed her a small envelope and walked away.

Sarah stared at the blue envelope she'd been handed. She quickly placed it in her lap.

"What's that?" The two voices on either side of her asked in unison.

Having a feeling where the note originated, Sarah desperately needed some privacy. Nodding to Rick and Mrs. E, she stated, "You two start eating. It's from Courtney. Let me just see what this is all about."

"You have to eat, too." Mrs. E. pointed to Sarah's salad on the table.

"I will once I see to this. Excuse me." Sarah rose from her chair and walked to the open area by the bar. She stopped, with her back to the dining area, and opened the envelope. She withdrew the blue Agency issued stationary which read in bold, black letters:

BATHROOM – 10 MINUTES

"The Eagle's pretty upset. You best be prepared." Sarah whirled around and found Sam Tanner standing behind her, his hands on his hips.

"I figured she'd be. I've some explaining to do."

"That, my dear, is an understatement, and you know it. She's invested a lot in you and your training. If it's something serious, she'll understand. Sarah, I've never known her not be fair. But consider this a warning. She'll go down fighting to keep you." A small grin broke out on the man's face.

Sarah brushed a kiss onto the beloved man's cheek. "Thanks, Chief." With Sam's warning in mind, she walked back to the table. Ravenous, she wondered how much dinner she could wolf down before the showdown with her boss.

It felt like the longest ten minutes of her life. Half way through the best piece of prime rib she'd ever tasted, she excused herself. She was grateful the meal had come. Rick hadn't brought up the infamous note, not that she'd thought he would in mixed company. Not here, with prying eyes and ears. Knowing she dodged a bullet, she breathed a sigh of relief.

Grabbing her purse, she pushed chair back and stood up.

Rick inquired, "Where are you going now? We have things to talk about."

Check that, she thought. Maybe she wasn't out of the woods...yet.

"If you don't mind, I have need of the ladies' room. I'll be back shortly." Sarah quickly turned her back on the table, nodded to a few people she knew, and made her way to the rest room. Her heart started to race, her hands felt clammy. When she hadn't received an immediate reply to her letter of resignation, she dreaded what would come - and when!

* * *

Coming out of the stall, she rinsed her hands, drying them with the decorative paper towels set on the side of the sink. It was then the end stall door opened. Elizabeth Hallock walked out. Her boss strode towards her. "No. You're safe... for now. You obviously know we can't discuss anything here." The woman wore an extremely determined look on her face. "However, the time has come to discuss your letter, Agent Adams."

"Yes, Director." Sarah swallowed the lump in her throat. The lady could be intimidating when she wanted to be. And this was one of those times.

"A private jet will be waiting for you on the National Guard side of the tarmac at Gabreski at 0600 tomorrow morning.

You'll come to D.C. Pack your bags. Enough for one week should do it. I have one last, short assignment for you."

"But...I thought..." Shocked, Sarah struggled with her words.

"Then, and only then, when the assignment is complete, will I accept your resignation." Elizabeth summarily dismissed her by pulling open the ladies' room door and walking out.

Shit! Shit! Shit! Sarah pulled out her cell phone and placed a call to Shelby.

Her friend answered on the second ring. "A 9-1-1 so soon?"

"I've got big-time troubles. I'm going to use you as an excuse to get out of here."

"Exactly how am I playing into you escaping from you know who?"

Sarah wasn't ready to get into the specifics. "I'm telling people your car broke down and you need a ride because you were called in for an emergency shift. Can you be at my apartment in fifteen minutes?"

"Cool."

"Oh, yeah? What's so cool about this?

There was a giggle at the other end of the phone. "I like playing at being a secret agent."

Sarah had no time for Shelby's antics. "Just get your butt to my apartment and plan on spending the night." Sarah barked into her phone. "It will take a few minutes for the valet to get my car."

"Copy that, boss."

"Say what?" Sarah pulled her phone away from her ear and stared at it. She loved Shelby's sense of humor, but now was not the right time.

"I always wanted to be a spy." Shelby laughed again. "I'll probably be there before you. I'll put on the hot cocoa. From the sound of things, I get the feeling it's going to be a long night."

"You got that right." Sarah ended the call and stood looking into the ornate mirror above the bathroom's sink. She'd had a nagging suspicion all day that the Director would pull her aside. But the woman followed protocol to the letter, and one would never discuss anything anywhere near mixed company.

Her thoughts were a mass of contradictions. When she accepted the invitation, wasn't her purpose to see if Rick showed he was capable of being the loving, romantic man who seemed to want a happily ever after? Or would he brush her aside as he'd done all the others before her? Now, she'd never find out. Even worse, her plans to leave Hampton Beach had to be put on hold. She swore under her breath.

Sarah couldn't believe the Director had attached strings to her letter of resignation. As an agent she had to follow orders. She'd normally come out swinging, but, given her circumstances, she'd no energy left to fight back. The Director held all the cards. And how difficult could the assignment be once Sarah explained her circumstances?

With her back straight and her head held high, she walked out of the ladies' room and made her way back to the dining room. But she didn't sit down at the table and finish her meal. Everyone was busy chattering away but stopped when she reappeared.

"Oh, good. You're back. Kate and John just brought John Jr. over. You missed him." Mrs. E. took one look at her. Sarah saw the concern in her eyes. "Something's not right. What took you so long? Are you okay?"

Sarah felt she'd done nothing but lie constantly throughout the last several weeks. Sick of doing so, she had no choice. "Listen, I've got to go. Shelby called and needs a lift to Riverhead. Her car broke down and she's got to sub on the night shift." She reached for the small favor of candies by her seat and tucked her purse under her arm. "I'll touch base soon."

Unfortunately, she wasn't going to be allowed a hasty exit. Rick stood up and grabbed her by the arm. "You can't leave yet." She attempted to withdraw her arm from his hand without causing a scene, but his grip was too strong. "I thought you and I..." From the tone in his voice, the man was trying to keep his temper in check in front of everyone.

She looked down to where Rick laid his hand on her arm. He immediately dropped it to his side. She then glanced up, her eyes taking in one last look of the man she loved. God, she thought, you are really fucked up. Her emotions were a mass of contradictions. "I'm sorry," she apologized to her tablemates. "I've got to go. Shelby's waiting for me."

Turning her back on Rick, she quickly hustled her way out of the room like Cinderella running from her Prince at the stroke of midnight.

CHAPTER NINE

Washington, D.C.
Oct. 1st
9 a.m.

The quiet on the Director's jet was just what Sarah needed after the grilling she received from Shelby when the two talked into the wee hours of the morning. Without violating protocol, she'd no choice but to take Shelby into her confidence. She described the "basics" of what she did and about her impending trip to D.C.

Leaving out the mandate of completing one last assignment, Sarah trusted Shelby wouldn't betray her. If anyone asked where Sarah went, Shelby would only say she'd requested time off from the beach club if they hadn't already heard via the "townie" grapevine. That and going on vacation were decent reasons for being absent from Hampton Beach.

After a small catnap, the two rose at dawn. Shelby had her to the airport in record time. The two said their good-byes, making promises to be in touch. Sarah knew full well it would be impossible to do so. Waiting for clearance to take off, she looked out the jet's window. A lone tear trickled down her cheek. Setting her problems aside, Sarah could only focus on only one person - the woman awaiting her in D.C.

After a ninety-minute flight, Sarah was now comfortably ensconced in a club chair in the sitting area of the Director's home office where the woman entertained her guests with her typical fare of Earl Grey tea and scones. She scanned her surroundings. It was four years since she last sat across from the massive mahogany desk on the other end of the cherry paneled room. Newly recovered from the shot to her leg she'd received on assignment while in London, and cleared by the Agency doctor, it was here the Director spelled out the need for her presence in Hampton Beach. Her journey home began, although trying to be "the real Sarah Adams" while working "undercover" became extremely stressful at times. She chuckled to herself. There were times she hadn't known which role she was playing, or "which end was up" as Gram would say.

"What are you laughing at?"

Sarah turned towards the masculine voice at the door. Sam Tanner. In all the years she worked for the Director, he'd become a father figure to her as well as other agents. Sam was the one who'd turned her nest egg of money into gold. How could she ever show him how deeply indebted she was for his friendship, his financial knowledge, and for always, always, having her back - especially on the few times she and the Director went nose to nose during the two operations on Long Island.

"Nothing in particular. Just remembering. I expected to see you both waiting for me when I got here. I hope she won't mind I made myself at home. Juanita's making tea…and your favorite, chocolate chips scones."

The sixty-four-year old man, his salt and pepper hair cut short military style, stood proud and tall as he strode towards her. "You didn't take the chair?" He winked at her, his eyes twinkling.

Sarah got the joke, shaking her head back and forth. "No. I decided I'd sit here first. Maybe by being here and not over there…" she pointed to the formal desk area, encased by four floor-to-ceiling windows, "I will feel more relaxed before I have to explain my side of the resignation before she goes ballistic. I've a feeling I'm in for the grilling of a lifetime."

Sam sat his tall frame on the sofa opposite her. "Elizabeth just wants answers. Your letter, to be honest…Well, I thought she was going to have a heart attack when she read the letter. Sarah, she's a tough old broad, but, as God is my witness, she actually burst into tears. But you did not hear that from me."

"I'll be honest with her, Sam. Lord knows I owe it to her… and you. She's been my boss and confidant. What would I have done without her when my folks died so tragically? She had faith in me when I didn't have faith in myself. However, contrary to what's she indicated, I'm not going out on another mission. I can't. There are reasons."

Sam had always been a hard one to read. He'd been trained to mask his emotions. But at that moment she spied a small facial tic of surprise at her defiance.

"Mark my words, Sarah. The Eagle's not going to give you a choice. Your area of expertise is..."

A small woman with a tray of coffee, tea and scones entered the room, placing her bounty on the coffee table. "Senorita Sarah. Bien?"

Sarah stood and gave the woman a warm hug. "Si, Juanita."

Staring into Juanita's black eyes, she noticed the woman looking her over. "You have been sick. Your face. It is pale, no? There's something in su ojos."

Praying Juanita wouldn't notice she hadn't tucked her blouse into the waist of her skirt, part of her standard Agency issued suit, she replied, "I've been feeling a bit off. But, I'm much better now. You look..."

"I hope everyone is done with reunions and kissy-kisses. We've worked to do." The woman of the hour waltzed through the open door, staring down the room's three occupants.

Elizabeth Hallock had arrived. She always had a unique way of making an entrance. Juanita gave Sarah one last hug and left the room, closing the door behind her. Thinking she'd be instructed to take her choice of beverage and go sit in "the chair" Sam referred to earlier, Sarah was surprised to see the Director stroll to her desk and pick up a piece of paper. She then walked back to the seating area. She sat next to Sam, a wide smile on her face. Her demeanor, one hundred and eighty degrees opposite that in the ladies' room, surprised Sarah. The Director pointed to the club chair on the other side of the coffee table and Sarah immediately sunk into its comfortable cushions.

"Tea, Sarah? There's Baileys." Elizabeth set about pouring the hot, steaming beverage into one of the cups on the table.

"Tea, please. No Baileys." Sarah eyed her boss as the woman demurely showed her softer side. Again, she was perplexed at the cat and mouse game that seemed to be occurring. *All right. Play along with the polite conversation and wait for the shoe to drop.*

Surprise did register on both the Director and Sam's faces. "You've never turned down Baileys before," Elizabeth said. "It's a family ritual. What's wrong?"

Sarah grew flushed, thinking of all the deceptions of the last few weeks. "If you must know, Doc Davis put me on a vitamin regiment. He said it would best if I stick to an alcohol-free diet."

Elizabeth, having filled Sarah's cup with tea and two sugars, passed it across the table. Sarah accepted the decorated English tea cup and placed it on the table in front of her afraid her hands would betray her nervousness by shaking. But her boss eyed her with suspicion. "You've seen Doc Davis? Protocol, Agent Adams, dictates you report to an Agency doctor, does it not?" The Director paused, deep in thought. Then, she asked, "Did you see Doc before or after you wrote me your letter of resignation?" The woman emphasized the last four words.

"I…I… honestly don't recall." She really didn't. Sarah finally reached for her cup, sat back in her chair, and took a sip of the tea. The warmth of the hot liquid hitting her stomach was just what she needed. It immediately seemed to calm her nerves. Thinking back to the day she paid Doc a visit, she assumed her letter had arrived in D.C. There certainly was enough time for the letter to travel from Hampton Beach to the nation's capitol. As a matter of fact, she'd received proof from the Post Office since she'd sent the letter via certified mail. The green receipt she'd received in return as proof of arrival had been signed by someone in the HR department, not by a member of the Director's immediate staff. That would certainly explain why Sarah sat on pins and needles awaiting the call that never came. "Madame Director, with all due respect, I didn't think feeling sluggish and tired required a visit all the way to D.C. I simply thought I was coming down with something. As to my letter, I truly thought you'd received it. I awaited your call for the time when we could discuss my resignation."

The Director took several sips of tea and leveled a telling look at her. "As I told you last evening, I'll accept your resignation after you complete one small job."

"And how long do you envision it will take?" The more the word "assignment" was mentioned, the more nervous Sarah became. She stared at the two people sitting across from her. There had better be a good explanation as to why the Director wouldn't sign off as she had done for several of Sarah's colleagues. Why was she being denied the same right to up and leave? She'd fulfilled her contract.

"No more than a week…I think."

Sarah eyed her boss skeptically.

Sam, who'd been in the process of taking a swallow of coffee from his mug, started to choke. Elizabeth withdrew his mug from his hands and slapped him on the back. "Oh, for heaven's sake. Haven't I told you not to drink so fast?"

Sarah grew anxious upon seeing the look that passed between the two people across from her. "Why do I have a feeling I'm not going to like what you have in store for me? Much less where I might be going." Adrenaline coursed through her body. Her anxiety level shot through the roof. She bolted from her chair. She didn't care if she'd be in trouble. Manual Rule #22 stated one *never* stood up before the Director instructed one to do so.

Sarah walked around her chair trying to put some distance from the Director and Sam. She began to pace back and forth on the plush Oriental carpet. Two pairs of eyes followed her every move. "You two have to level with me." She put up her hand, palm out to thwart any retorts. "Don't point out how much I owe you. That's a given. What I don't get is why I can't simply bow out as others have done? Operation Hallock Farm is in the books. Signed, sealed, and delivered. There's nothing presently happening in the hamlets requiring any kind of Agency intervention." Sarah stopped to look at her companions. Did she have to beg for them to see she wanted a simple end to her career? "I need to rest. When you count it up, I've had eight days off in *eleven* years? Eight! My contract allows me to resign and/or retire after ten. The vetting's taken place so technically I can walk away."

Sarah watched her two superiors exchange looks.

Elizabeth held the paper in her hand she'd retrieved from her desk. "You're correct, but sometimes the manual doesn't cover every situation. Once done, this…" she waved what Sarah assumed to be her contract in the air, "will be null and void. Then, you're free. I give you my word, I won't stand in your way. Right now, it's your knowledge of art that's desperately sought. There's been a heist of a group of valuable paintings from a collector living outside of London…a supposed heist."

Sarah took a step forward, intrigued. Any thought of terminating her Agency's contract was temporarily forgotten and pushed to the back of her mind. "Supposed? What do you mean? The heist either happened or it didn't."

"All will be explained in good time." Elizabeth wore a satisfied smile on her face. Great. Her boss knew just the right words to bait her hook, line and sinker. "Our problem seems to be the one reporting the crime - a former MI6..."

"MI6? That's Scotland Yard," Sarah cringed inwardly. There was a manual rule somewhere about interrupting the Director. "Are we to undergo a joint operation?" Her body and mind automatically shifted into Agent mode. Sarah was so focused on what the Director said she didn't hear the door to the office open.

"I'm here and at your service, Director, as requested and, please take note, I'm actually on time. Hi, Sam. I figured you'd be here."

Hearing the familiar masculine voice, Sarah stood stunned and watched as Rick saluted the Director and Sam. Her legs suddenly felt like jelly. She grabbed for the back of the club chair to maintain her balance and her heart hammered in her chest. Her vision blurred as her head felt weird. She managed to spew out, "What the hell is he doing here?" She looked to the Director, and then at Sam, for an explanation.

"Sarah, we were about to explain," Sam said, shooting a side look at Elizabeth as if to say, "I told you so."

Sarah kept a strong hold onto the back of the chair. Shell shocked, she didn't miss the look on Rick's face when it dawned on him she was present in the room. His expression mimicked her own. He exclaimed, "What the...?" The man was as shell-shocked as she was, but his eyes never left hers. "Sarah! Why are you here at the compound?" He wagged his index finger at her. "You've got some serious explaining to do. You just ran off and left me last night. We were going to talk, if you recall."

For once, Sarah prayed the Director or Sam would step in to soothe the savage beast. And they did. Elizabeth rose and made her way to stand near Sarah. Sam made his way to be by Rick's side.

A huge knot of tension built in her stomach and perspiration broke out on her upper lip. The man's unexpected appearance had her mind racing in a thousand different directions. She lost focus on those around her. Blinking her eyes, she realized the room was starting to spin. She quickly pushed the Director aside. She hoped she'd make it into the chair before her legs gave out.

Sarah made it within inches of her destination. Her last thoughts, before the darkness claimed her, were for her baby. As she dropped to the floor, Rick, Elizabeth and Sam stood rooted in place, horror etched on their faces. When she hit the cushioned carpet, her head narrowly missed the coffee table.

It was a good thing Sarah wasn't conscious of the flurry of activity of the trio attempting to tend to her. As they rushed to help her, each, in turn, shouting commands at the other. Oh, if they only knew.

CHAPTER TEN

A cool cloth gently caressed the side of Sarah's face. As her eyes fluttered open, she tried in vain to make out her surroundings. Unfortunately, she was totally disoriented. Where am I?

From where she lay on a bed, as her blurry vision rapidly disappeared, she spied Juanita. The woman's sharp black eyes assessed her, her face showed signs of worry. The Spanish woman crooned, "Hush, Senorita." Sarah attempted to raise herself up onto her elbows, but Juanita placed the damp cloth in her hand on the bedside table and gently pushed her back onto the comfortable bed. "No. No." She clucked like a mother hen. "You must lie still. You must rest." Bending over the bed, she lovingly touched Sarah's cheek, and then felt her forehead. Satisfied she didn't have a fever, Juanita pulled her hand away.

With her body totally depleted, Sarah's mind drew a total blank. She wanted answers. "Juanita, what happened? Why am I here?" Again, she attempted to rise, but her boss's house-keeper placed her hands upon Sarah's shoulders, lightly pushing her back into a deep mound of pillows. Juanita drew a blue flowered comforter over her, tucking her in as a mother would her child at bedtime. Once more eyeing her surroundings, it finally dawned on Sarah she was in the guest bedroom reserved for visiting dignitaries.

From a Queen Anne's chair, in the corner of the room, came the soft southern drawl of her boss. She sounded frazzled and worried when she spoke. "You're in bed because you fainted. I've had Doc Davis on the phone." The Director rose from where she'd been sitting and walked across the room. Sitting down upon the edge of the queen size bed, she said, "From the little he's told me, I now have a pretty good idea what's going on."

Still dizzy, Sarah closed her eyes and shook her head from side to side as if by doing so she could deny the inevitable. Tears streamed from the corners of her eyes and onto the white pillowcase. Everything had been so well planned out days ago. She thought she'd aligned her life perfectly. Everything in the past always went according to plan. Then, she'd been summoned to D.C. and her life imploded.

To make matters worse, as if another assignment thrown in the works wasn't enough, Rick had showed up in the Director's home! What was he doing here? If she only could bury under the covers and stay locked in this gloriously decorated room with Juanita to care for her for the next six months. Life would be golden.

"Director, might you and I have a moment of privacy?" Sarah's voice trembled, barely coming out as a whisper.

Elizabeth Hallock cocked her head towards the bedroom door. "Juanita. Please bring Sarah some tea and toast. I think she could use some sustenance in her stomach. Once she's fed, we'll come back downstairs."

"Absolutely." Picking up the wet washcloth, Juanita exited the room, closing the door firmly behind her.

Sarah bolted upright now that Juanita wasn't there to force her to stay put. Her eyes locked on the Director's. "Madam Director. Please. You *must* trust me on this. I can't face Rick. If this job requires Rick and I to partner up…" Sarah drew in several deep cleansing breaths and exhaled. "I implore you to choose someone else."

Elizabeth said nothing for a few seconds. Then the woman took her phone from her jacket pocket and perched her trademark eyeglasses on the end of her nose. Scrolling through a list of contacts, the woman pressed one particular key. Doc's voice came through loud and clear on the first ring.

"She's awake, Lizzie?" Doc asked.

"Yes. I ordered her a bit of food. I don't think she's eaten today. Howard, I need her. Especially her expertise."

Sarah listened intently as the Director and Doc discussed her as if she wasn't in the room.

"Lizzie Hallock." Doc's tone was firm. "Listen carefully. I'll clear her for one week. Period. Based on the task you said needs doing, she'll be fine. But, please rethink your plans. Rick brings a great deal of added stress…" Doc's voice trailed off. Was the man pondering what to say or not to say? "Did she impart that I told her to go away for a month for rest and relaxation?"

Elizabeth's spine stiffened. The lady didn't like being kept in the dark on any matter. Nor was she used to someone telling her to back off. "I don't tell you how to run your clinic, Howard. Don't tell me how to operate the CIA."

Sarah had enough of being left out of the conversation. "Doc? Please tell her no to my working. I can't handle the stress it might bring on." Sarah's eyes took in the body language of the woman who sat on her bed. An awful feeling settled in her gut. It was going to be the Director's way whether Sarah or Doc liked it or not.

"We discussed the need for full transparency, didn't we, Sarah?" Was Doc going over to the dark side? Sarah stared at the phone in disbelief. She thought he'd be her strongest ally. "You *are* strong and capable, and, above all, you're healthy. The Director informed me there's nothing that requires extreme physical activity, if that's why you're worried. You'll be fine. But, I'm not about to get in the middle of this and pit you against your boss. I understand you've got your resignation riding on this last job. You're well enough to take it on and then be done."

Sarah shot a look at the Director. The woman wore a sly grin on her face. As far as the Director was concerned it was "mission accomplished". Sarah lay back onto the pillows, her brain reeling. She had no way out. She was stuck so she might as well resign herself to the fact and get the week over with.

"Be honest with me given the circumstances. How do you feel, Sarah?" Doc inquired.

She replied, trying to keep the disgust from her voice, but failed to do so. "A bit shaky. I want this over and done with. Then, I'll take that vacation. Apparently you must be on speed dial should I need you." Elizabeth nodded her head in the affirmative as she continued her conversation. "I'll do as you said about the vitamins and the eating. The Director started to explain the job when Rick walked in. I think the mere sight of him brought on a panic attack and my body gave out."

Doc's voice crackled through the phone. "Lizzie, I implore you to listen to Sarah. Do not make judgments." His tone turned gruff. "And for the record, I'm done playing spy. When this job's over, delete my number from your phone." There was a resounding click. Doc had hung up on the Director.

There was a light knock at the bedroom door.

"Come in!" The Director instructed. When the door didn't open, she got up from the bed and opened the door herself. Juanita stood in the hall, her hands carrying a tray of food. "Oh, Juanita. Thank you. You know where to put it."

The housekeeper walked around the foot of the bed bearing a tray of items - a pot of Earl Grey tea, toast and selected jams. She placed it on a small circular table surrounded by two Windsor chairs near a large bay window. The early afternoon sun shone in, warming the alcove.

"That looks lovely. Close the door on your way out. Juanita could you see to it Rick and Sam get some lunch?" Elizabeth wore a brighter smile than she had five minutes earlier. But, of course, the woman had got what she wanted, Sarah thought.

Elizabeth stood up from the bed once Juanita left. She offered her arm to Sarah for support. Sarah sat up, swung her legs over the edge of the bed, and placed her arm through the crook of the Director's elbow. With her feet firmly planted on the floor, she stood up, making sure she had her sea legs. Nodding assurance it was okay to proceed, Sarah walked slowly over to the small sitting area holding onto the Director's arm.

Once seated, Sarah took in the view from the bedroom windows. Elizabeth Hallock's home was one of the grander mansions situated just off Embassy Row. She had served as the Director of the prestigious agency for several consecutive presidential administrations. Before that, she spent twenty-five plus years working her way up the ranks from a field operative in the European theater, with Sam Tanner as her partner, to finally being in command of the CIA headquarters in Langley, VA. The mansion reflected her status amongst the D.C. elite, as well as a home away from home – Hallock Farm in Hampton Beach.

Still a bit rattled and unsure of herself, Sarah took another deep breath. Her boss held out a cup of steaming tea to her. Taking the delicate cup in both hands, she first placed it on the circular table, not quite trusting her trembling hands to bring it directly to her mouth without spilling its contents on the pristine linen tablecloth. Her stomach growled as if on cue as she reached for a piece of buttered toast. With gusto she picked up the knife on her napkin and spread strawberry jam on the slice of bread, then ravenously took several bites.

When Sarah looked up, she saw the Director's face turning a distinct shade of red. Was the infamous leader of the CIA blushing? It was evident the topic she wanted to discuss was out of her comfort zone. Sarah sat back, watched and waited. "Sarah, dear. I can't read blood results and interpret testing. But when the bottom of Doc's notes said 'pre-natal vitamins prescribed', it didn't take a rocket scientist to put two and two together. No wonder you wanted out. Now things make sense."

Sarah picked up the dainty cup with both hands and took a long swallow to wash down the toast that stuck in her throat. *The lady knows how to get right to the point. Face it. You were going to tell her and Sam right before Rick walked in the door.*

She placed her hand on her belly. "Yes. I'm pregnant." She immediately put her hand in the air to thwart any forthcoming comments. For once, she wanted to be the one in charge. "I might as well tell you Rick is the father. It happened the night of Courtney and Thomas's wedding. One night. Period. Did I plan it? Absolutely not! The whole night was a huge mistake on my part. Doc's made me aware of my options. You need to know I've chosen to keep this baby and move on, on-my-own." She emphasized the last three words and continued. "I want to severe my ties with the Agency and move away from Hampton Beach. I've a plan to bring my grandparents with me. They don't know yet so I ask you respect my privacy and right to tell them." Sarah stopped, took another sip of tea and bit into the delicious piece of bread. She was surprised her boss didn't interrupt. "Enough about my pregnancy. I don't think I need to reiterate I have real reservations about being forced into this final job. I'll follow orders. However, I will not work with *him*."

The Director crossed her arms over her ample bosom and sighed. "Child, don't you think Rick has the right to know the truth? Trust me when I say I know a lot about keeping secrets from those I've loved. Nothing good ever comes from it. Ever."

What could the Director possibly have to hide? Were there secrets in her personal closet as well? There'd been a rumor circulating several years ago she and Sam had had a love affair during one of their operations. Sarah was brought out of her musings upon hearing her boss's voice.

"Have you thought about the future? What if this child wants to meet his biological father? What then? Everything could backfire." Elizabeth leaned back in her chair. Time seemed to stand still as the woman awaited Sarah's response. Sarah was determined not to get into a debate over what she considered a very personal issue.

"If you want me, there will be terms." Sarah stated adamantly.

Elizabeth sat up straight, her eyes widening. "There is no negotiating when given a direct order."

Sarah leaned forward in her seat and stared down her boss. "If you can guarantee we will have minimal contact, I'll work with...him." She spat out the last word. "I'm going to guess Rick must have some connection to the heist you've referred to. But be fair warned, I am out in one week as you promised. I'll impart whatever expertise is needed to complete the job." Sarah felt she'd firmly stood her ground. "You, Madame Director, are honor bound to release me at the end."

Elizabeth wiped her mouth with the flowered napkin and rose from the table. For the first time that day, the woman seemed flustered. Sarah had expected a lengthy retort. Instead, the woman eyed her with another look of motherly concern

and then directed, "Get yourself together. Don't be too long. There's much to be done. I'll see you downstairs."

Sarah stood up slowly, feeling more steady on her feet. That small bit of food had done the trick. "Give me fifteen minutes and I'll meet you in your office. And... thank you."

The Director was almost to the door when she turned and stated, "I'll honor your request, Sarah. Rick and his team are the other parties the Agency is helping out. But, need I reiterate things don't always go as planned?"

A chill rushed down Sarah's spine seeing the door close behind the Director. Halloween was thirty days away. Maybe she'd better take her Princess Leia costume out from its hiding place in the closet. It seems Darth Vader just walked out the door.

* * *

"My IT team traced two accounts of the suspect to the Cayman Islands. There were several recent deposits, making us wonder if some paintings were sold on the black market. But, we've no proof if that's true or not. When the team finished the forensic accounting and traced his activities, that's when I knew I had to call you. What has Scotland Yard offered? Anything to fill in the blanks?" Rick had thought the trip to D.C. would be a waste of valuable time. He should have followed his gut and gone to London and been on the ground with his team. But that thought flew out the window when he'd walked into the Director's office and seen Sarah. If given the choice, he'd pass the case off to someone else within his agency and move on now that he had her in his sights, but he was too entrenched in the sting operation to back away.

"Scotland Yard? I hear there's been a heist and you need my expertise."

Sarah! Rick's head swung around and spotted the woman who'd consumed his thoughts for the last hour. As she walked further into the office, she still looked a bit pale, but she was rubbing her hand together, obviously ready to get down to business. He was amazed she seemed so up-beat considering what he witnessed. The hardest part was going to be keeping his hands off her. He warred within himself how to do just that while she was upstairs readying herself to come back down to join them.

His sixth sense told him something wasn't right. Yesterday, when she vehemently denied being ill, she'd swept the issue under the rug. Based on what had recently occurred, she wasn't telling the truth and that had him worried. Big time. Couple that with not being able to erase the image in his mind of having to carry her limp body from the office to a bedroom. Why had she fainted? His mind reverted to Mrs. Eckart's comments about Sarah's visit to see the town doctor and the fact she was headed off on vacation. One thing was for damn sure, Rick was determined to find what Sarah was hiding since she'd be by his side night and day for the next week.

With Sarah and the Director upstairs, Sam summarized how Sarah's knowledge of art would integrate into what Rick's team uncovered. The character involved, the collector and former MI-6 agent, sounded like a sleazy bastard. Glancing again at the woman who waited inside the doorway, Rick knew two things. He would never forgive himself if anything happened to her on his watch. And they were, like it or not, going to talk about the note.

Seeing Sam stand up, Rick stood as well. Maps and piles of folders lay strewn across its top. Pulling out the black Windsor chair, he tried not to seem over eager; he simply pointed to the middle chair. Their private showdown would come later. "Sarah. Please sit. Take a load off."

As he lowered himself into the chair on her left, he couldn't help but seeing her eye him suspiciously.

After digging through a pile of paper on the desk, Sam finally sat in the remaining chair. "We need to go over a few details before we head out."

Sarah jumped in, not giving Sam time to continue. "I want you both to know I've made my opinion about this op very clear to the Director." She turned in his direction, leveling a look that inferred he was persona nongratis. "Our 'misunderstanding' will not be discussed. Do I myself clear?" All Rick could do, with three pairs of eyes staring at him, was to nod his head in agreement. This wasn't the time or the place for the conversation he and Sarah had to have. But there would be, come hell or high water. "I'm here solely to help you with an art heist. The Director promised me I'd me done in one week...tops."

A bit stunned with the tone Sarah took with her superiors, Rick leaned back in his chair and stared at her. He replied in return, "I know. The Director made that clear to Sam and me when she briefed us. My team thinks the time frame is doable. Understand, Sarah, since this heist occurred overseas, the Director offered me the Agency's services, especially knowing the specifics and who was involved. Your background in art history will be a tremendous asset, Agent Adams." *Make her think you can keep things professional between you...for now.*

Sarah's nostrils flared. "Don't placate me. Let's just get this over with."

Shocked, Rick couldn't help but arch his eyebrows given her tone. Sam and the Director had the same reaction.

Sarah questioned the group. "I take it we'll set up Command Central in London? I'm quite familiar with the city. The contacts I made will come in handy. I'm assuming I'll be taking point?"

Man, the lady was direct and focused when it came to the job.

"Agent Adams!" The Director's fist met the massive wooden desk in front of her, the sound reverberated throughout the room. "Listen and learn. Sam filled Rick in on the major details. He's in possession of the materials necessary for the sting. The two of you can go over them while you're on your way to Easthampton. Our plane leaves within the hour."

Sarah gave a swift shake of her head as if she hadn't heard correctly. "I beg your pardon. Did you say Easthampton? You mentioned MI6 and Scotland Yard. We're not headed to England?"

The Director shook her head. "No, we're not. My agents in New York traced the stolen contraband with the help of Interpol. A former operative I worked with years ago had a problem with the collector's statement to the British police, among other issues. That really got the ball rolling. Believe it or not, the paintings have been smuggled out of Britain and are here in the States. Our intelligence has traced them to somewhere in the vicinity of Easthampton, New York."

With his hands folded in his lap, Rick thought it would be best to let the Director deal with Sarah. Out of the corner of his eye, he watched his "partner" shake her head in disbelief.

The CIA Chief took a brief moment to glance at a piece of paper on her desk. "Sam and I can't believe the man had the balls to up and move the paintings – the ones he filed a theft report for. What works in our favor, however, is there's to be a huge auction - a fundraiser, in two weeks to maintain…"

Sarah drummed her fingers on the arms of her chair, her lips were pursed, and her eyes targeted the Director. There was a frown on her face. "Excuse me, but you told me this op would require *one* week."

The Director commenced tapping a pen on her desk, her eyes on Sarah. Clearly, the head of the Agency was attempting to keep her temper in check. "Yes, I did say that. However, there's been a slight change in plans." Sarah sat up straight in her chair, no doubt getting ready to do battle. But with one dagger like glare from her boss, Sarah backed down. "As I was saying, if you'd will let me finish, the fundraiser is for the Easthampton Arts Program, a unique program for local students in the area. That's where you come in, Sarah. We're almost ninety-nine percent positive somebody in Easthampton is going to help our thief get the art out of the country. We've no idea why he transported the stolen works to the States from Britain, but somehow there's a connection to the fundraiser. We need you to verify what we believe our agents and Rick's team have located. Our confidential informant at Gabreski has confirmed there's a private jet set to fly out to JFK the night of the auction."

Rick noted Sarah spent time during the briefing writing a few notes on a pad of paper. He watched her circle several items on her list. A stickler for details, she stated, "But that's two weeks from now. Why would anyone file a flight plan that early? It's a red flag."

Sam stepped in. "Exactly what I thought. Remember, a small airfield was built in Easthampton several years ago. It's easy to get from there to Gabreski and then onto JFK. We've got agents spanned out from Hampton Beach all the way to Montauk. They're searching for planes that might have been rented. There's several locals on our payroll who've been in touch as well."

Elizabeth Hallock pointed first to Rick and then to Sarah. "You both will attend that fundraiser."

"What? You can't be serious." The woman beside him defiantly crossed her arms over her chest and sighed in disgust.

For once he agreed, Rick thought. When Sam described how his team would cooperate with the Agency's plan of action, he'd become more confused and perplexed. Rick shook his head in denial. *My company investigates the books and locates the monies. Then, the clients take what I find from there. How is possible I've landed in two CIA ops with my boots on the ground within six months?*

"I certainly am serious." This time the Director's tone was a tad harsh, but the woman by his side wasn't giving in without a fight.

Sarah pointed to Sam and then to the woman who sat opposite her in the leather wing chair. "Well, then let me point out you've one slight problem with your game plan."

"And exactly what would that be, Agent Adams?" Elizabeth leaned back, her dark eyes clearly fixated on Sarah. The Eagle looked ready to take her protégé down a peg or two. Rick could only imagine what was reeling through Sarah's mind.

"You know I'm known in the Hamptons as the manager of the Sunfish. What excuse are you going to have to explain Rick's presence? His only visibility thus far was Courtney's wedding. He was totally invisible during Operation Hallock Farm. He's not a known fixture in the Hampton social scene. My being with him will raise eyebrows. I'm just a 'townie' for my cover. I don't fit in either."

"I believe that could be easily remedied," Rick interrupted, a plan hatching in his brain. The Director, Sam and Sarah focused their attention onto him. Was the room getting warmer, or was he just feeling as if he'd put himself in the hot seat. His idea was a viable solution to their problem. "I'll take Sarah as my plus one. This will be an invite only affair of people with a lot of money to spend. Am I correct?"

The woman across the other side of the desk folded her hands, placing them on her desk. She brought her finger up and stroked her chin as she pondered his idea. "I believe you're onto something. The fundraiser is indeed by invitation only."

The woman beside him gasped, "No! I simply will not..." Sarah stopped. He raised his hand in the air like a child wanting to ask a question in the classroom. "*What* could you possibly offer up now, Einstein?"

"Agent Adams!" The Director barked and he watched as Sarah slinked back into her chair. The woman looked none too pleased. "Rick, what do you want to add? Your idea is superb. I wish I'd thought of it myself."

"Thanks. But an even better thought just dawned on me, one that might help Sarah and me out of difficult situations we might encounter down the road."

"I'm listening." The Director replied.

It was all or nothing. Go for it.

Rick watched as the look on Sarah's face told him she was finally resigned to the fact that no matter how much she argued, begged, or pleaded, the Director was going to have the final say. "Would it be possible for you to put a bolo out to the

Hallock clan? We're also going to need a false article printed up in the ***Hampton Times***."

"I certainly could do that." A devilish look crossed the woman's face. He could tell immediately they were on the same way length.

"What, pray tell, is this article going to say?" Sarah's question was laced with sarcasm.

A smug look appeared on his face, pleased he'd contributed to the Director's plan. "Simply that the reason you took your vacation was that you and I ran off to Vegas...and got married."

CHAPTER ELEVEN

Three days later

"We've been flying and driving for almost two and a half hours and you haven't said one word." Already having read the contents of the folder on his lap three times, Rick had waited patiently for Sarah to say something, anything. "I expected you'd blow when we landed at Gabreski and the Director and Sam left us alone and boarded their SUV entourage headed for Command Central."

Throughout the ninety-minute flight from D.C., Sarah focused solely on the briefing materials Rick shared with her, reading page after page after page. Wings down and on the ground in Hampton Beach, she'd brushed past him when she exited the plane, and climbed into the waiting limousine. "Pardon me for thinking our getting married was a good reason so you'd gain easier access to the upper class in Easthampton. That's what you wanted, wasn't it?"

"You haven't the faintest idea what you've done." His lady's voice was harsh and cold. "Everything would have worked out somehow." Sarah turned from looking out at the passing scenery of pine trees and stared him down.

Oh yeah. The lady was p-i-s-s-e-d, with a capital P.

She railed on. "Being your date would have sufficed. I would have had the invitation I needed. You've seen me in action, how I work. I need to get behind the scenes. Now, with our very public marriage announcement, all of Hampton society will be circling like vultures. Everyone will clamor for our constant attention to offer congratulations. Nice going, hot shot."

"Listen, I may not be an agent, but I do know how to send in a team in disguise to investigate a situation." Rick reached out and grabbed hold of her left hand. Sarah struggled to rid her hand from his, but he held on tight. No way was he going to let her stare out the window; he wanted her undivided attention. There were a multitude of things he had to get off his chest before arriving at the mansion he'd purchased several years ago. Elizabeth gave him the thumbs up when he told her his "summer cottage" was located in Easthampton, although he was certain she already knew. "Forgive me for thinking, if you were my wife, no one would question you. Money talks. Being my wife gives you status." Realizing what he'd just implied, he quickly added, "Not that being the manager of the prestigious Sunfish Beach Club isn't fine. Trust me. I'll make this right. I owe you." At least, when she'd climbed into the limo, she hadn't shied away, but taken the seat next to him. "Open your hand."

"Say what? Why would I want to do that?"

"Just do it. Like this." He demonstrated what he wanted her to do. He opened his other hand, palm side up. Rick released hers, pleasantly surprised she did as he requested.

"Exactly why am I doing this?"

"We have to make every detail real." Rick withdrew the box he acquired from Tiffany's from his coat pocket. When he snapped opened the box, he heard Sarah's soft gasp of surprise.

"That's the largest ring I've ever seen!" she exclaimed.

He slid the diamond ring onto the ring finger of her left hand. A perfect fit. "Will you marry me, Sarah Ann Adams?" Rick watched as her emotions got the better of her. *Well, this certainly wasn't what I'd planned on.* Her eyes grew watery, forcing her to pull a wadded-up tissue from her right coat pocket. "What's wrong? Mary, my secretary, said any woman would love it. You do like it, don't you?"

The woman bobbed her head up and down. Never did he think he'd see the day Sarah Adams was speechless. Even as she dabbed at her eyes, more tears trickled down both cheeks, but her eyes never left the ring.

"It's perfect," she whispered.

Rick thought he hadn't heard her correctly. "So, the ring is okay with you?"

"Yes." With tissue in hand, she blew her nose. "I'm so sorry. I cry all the time. Doc says it's all part of being… tired. But…"

"But what?"

"God. I don't believe you still don't see we still have a slight problem."

What had he missed? There was the proposal with the ring. Sarah had said, "Yes". Well, her nod of approval was as good as a verbal "yes" in his book. "Tell me. I've never done this. Things have to be in order so no one can question us. The Director even obtained a fake marriage license from Vegas in case someone goes digging." He took her chin in his hand and made her look him in the eye. "What is it? Tell me. Talk to me."

"A wedding ring, Rick. The Director's told the family we went to Vegas and got...*married*."

Slapping his forehead with his right hand, he exclaimed, "Damn! I thought I covered all the bases. What would I know? I've never been married, or ever thought how I'd ever do this up the right way." His comment made Sarah tug her hand from of his. Her body stiffened and she sat, staring straight ahead, saying nothing. *What the hell did I say?*

Suddenly, it dawned on him. *Dumb! Dumb! Dumb! You are one giant fool* with *shit for brains.* Taking his cell phone out of his jacket pocket, he pressed a button.

"What are you doing?"

Rick gave her thigh a reassuring squeeze. "Making things right. You made a valid point."

Sarah glanced back over at him. On her cheeks there was a smudge of black mascara from where she'd wiped away her tears. "Who are you calling? Didn't you pay attention to the Director's instructions? There's no communication with anyone until we reach base camp."

Rick didn't care about the rules right then. He wanted to please the woman by his side. To answer her, he pronounced, "Tiffany's. What kind of diamonds do you prefer? The sky's the limit..." A voice stopped him from saying anything else.

Instead, he focused on his call. "Rick Stockton here. Would Rita be available?"

Had he not seen Sarah using her finger to draw what she'd obviously dreamed of, he'd have missed her hushed whisper. "I want a ring with a diamond band of sapphires and diamonds interchanged all the way around."

A voice came on the other end of the line. With his eyes still on Sarah, he responded, "Hello, Rita. Looks like I'm going to need that wedding ring. Yes, imagine that…Yup, very quick." He winked at Sarah, but the woman was staring down at her hands in her lap. "Do you remember the Neil Lane you showed me the other day?"

Sarah's head snapped up, the shocked look on her face said it all. Didn't she know he could read her like a book ever since that fateful day back in March when they'd met?

"Yes. Size 6. I'll pay you double if you can jet it out to my Easthampton residence. 1450 Bishop Lane. I need a really big favor though. Can you get it to me by seven tonight? You can? Great! I'll be there to sign for it. Yes, use the same credit card. Rita, you're the best. He paused, listening to the woman on the other end of the line. "No. Thank you."

* * *

1450 Bishop Lane
Easthampton, Long Island

Talk about a turn of events. Sarah went to D.C. thinking she was fulfilling her final obligation that would allow her to terminate her job contract with the Agency. Then she would have been free. Instead, she was headed back to the Hamptons matched with the man she'd planned on running from originally!

She hadn't any real knowledge of diamond rings, except those on the fingers of the Hallock women. The one presently on her hand was a tad over the top, in her opinion. She was more of a simplistic kind of girl. But when push came to shove, she hated to admit to herself she really loved Rick's choice. Twisting the ring upside down, she pressed the diamond letting it cut into her palm. She hoped by doing so her unwanted romantic train of thoughts rolling around in her brain, since Rick announced they were getting "married", would evaporate.

Sarah Ann Adams, you should be ashamed of yourself. Thinking when he slipped the ring on your finger the man was proposing for real! God, what would Shelby say if you told her you actually described to him the wedding ring you dreamed of having one day. The one you both "oohed" and "aahed" over the night you were window- shopping at Zales. Focus! Quit dreaming and return to the real world. Engage that brain of yours. Do your job, play your part, find the art thieves, then, as planned get the hell of out Dodge.

Suddenly, Sarah realized the car had stopped. Her car door opened. Peeking out, she saw Sam Tanner standing at position as if he were the valet at the country club.

"Welcome home, Mrs. Stockton. So glad to be at your service." The man had a smirk on his face. She didn't find his delight with her predicament amusing. As she grabbed her purse and exited the limo, she shot a glare in his direction. Sarah had the perfect retort but kept it to herself. As she glanced back inside the vehicle, she found Rick's seat vacant. Now where had he gone?

"Honey! Over here." The man in question stood at the front door of his estate, the porch light shining on him. "I'm going to carry you over the threshold for good luck."

"Like hell you are," she growled.

Sam's voice caught her off guard. "Hush. You don't know who's listening. We've had to get a detail to keep the paparazzi at bay since the article went public. And no one in there," Sam pointed to Rick's house, "knows that the two of you are not married."

Grumbling under her breath, totally displeased by her current situation, she grudgingly climbed the stairs of the estate's entrance to her "husband". A strong pair of arms whisked her off her feet.

"Put me down this instant!" The man was incorrigible.

"No can do."

"Why ever not?"

"Because..."

Rick didn't have time to finish because the front door opened wide. Standing in the large foyer were several members of the Hallock clan – Helen and Robert, Matt and Megan, Courtney and Thomas, and Ethan. *How much more humiliating was this going to get?*

"Surprise!"

"Congratulations!"

"Bravo!"

"Well done, Rick!"

Helen brushed the members of her family aside to come and stand front and center. "Oh, I'm so happy for you both!" She clapped her hands together and danced a little jig. The woman was a diehard romantic. "Put her down, Rick. We want to hear all about your Vegas trip." Rick did as instructed, but held Sarah close to his side. His arm around her waist made her body tingle. The Hallock matriarch gushed, "We simply had to be the first to surprise you both and offer up hugs and good wishes. After all, you're family!"

A throat being cleared could be heard from behind the mass of well-wishers.

Helen's tone turned serious. "Oh, yes. I'm supposed to tell you Elizabeth filled us in about the fundraiser. You tell us whatever you need us to do." However, the woman couldn't on task for long. "Sarah, how could you just go off and elope on me? You know how I love to plan weddings! What did your grandparents have to say about gaining a grandson?"

Elizabeth came forward and interrupted her sister-in-law, shooting both Sarah and Rick a knowing look. "Sarah hasn't had a chance to talk to them yet, Helen. She'll do it tomorrow since it's late. I'm sure some at Beach House made sure she saw the article in the ***Hampton Times***. You can imagine Sarah will definitely need some time alone with them to explain."

Sarah sighed, relieved. Exactly how to phrase what she'd say to Gram and Pop played through on her mind on the plane ride back to the Hamptons.

Rick interjected, "Thanks so much for coming. Sarah and I truly appreciate it." Feeling him squeeze her elbow as if it was her cue to say something, Sarah was at a loss for words and merely nodded, pasting a smile on her face. "But, as the Director said, we've had an extremely long day and really could use some rest. Vegas was a bit much… Right, honey?" Sarah decided to say nothing about their imaginary trip to Vegas. The less said the better.

Knowing she had to acknowledge the crowd before her, she did her best to sound pleasant. "Ditto to what Rick said. We're very grateful to all of you. Maybe Mrs. H., to make up for us eloping, you can plan a nice party." Realizing what she'd inferred, Sarah immediately stopped talking.

"Everyone needs to leave. Now." Elizabeth's commanding voice rose above the din of chatter. "Sam gave you your burner phones. We'll meet once more before the auction. Robert," she turned to her brother. "I'll be sure you and Helen have adequate funds to access for the donation." She spoke to the entire crowd. "Remember to keep your eyes and ears open."

Yawning, Sarah turned to her boss. "I really need some sleep and get something to eat."

Taking one look at Sarah, Helen, as if on cue, quickly ushered her family past the "happy couple" and out the front door, closing it behind her with a final wave of good-bye.

Elizabeth turned to Rick. "That's quite some rock on her finger. Where's her wedding ring?"

"On its way from Tiffany's. Tell the guards at the gate to be on the look-out for Rita. She's jetting it in and should be here around eight."

"Good." Elizabeth pivoted, her eyes fell on Sarah. "Food and rest, yes?"

"Yes, Ma'am. I'm starving. I'll eat whatever you have, then just point me to my bedroom."

Rick's deep bass voice responded, "That would be on the second floor overlooking the ocean and pool."

What she would give to forget all about the man. However, this was his house. Plus, the assignment was a short one. She'd tolerate him for a week and finally be gone!

"I hope the bed is comfortable." Sarah countered, yawning even louder.

"It is. Mark my words. King size and very, very comfortable."

She stopped dead in her tracks at the kitchen doorway. The smells emanating from the steaming plates on the table made her mouth water and her stomach growl. But there was something inferred in what Rick had said. "Just how do you know that particular bed is comfortable?"

"Because it's mine."

Sarah bristled when she spied the man grinning like the Cheshire Cat. Oh, how she hated his arrogance! "Listen to me, Rick Stockton. *You* will sleep in *your* bed. I will sleep in a guest room that is as far from you as possible without being *on-the-beach.*"

"Enough! Both of you!" Elizabeth and Sam came to stand between them. "Dinner is served. We're hungry too. You both need to get a good night's rest. There's a lot of planning left to do."

The four sat down at the circular table in the breakfast nook. Sarah took in the size of the kitchen. "Seriously, you really own this house?" she asked.

Rick, who was shoveling food into his mouth, nodded his head in the affirmative.

A rock the size of Gibraltar, the wedding ring of her dreams, and… she was having his baby. Life sucked.

CHAPTER TWELVE

Hidden away in Thomas's study, with the Director's secure cell phone held to her ear, Sarah spied the clock on the wall. The phone call had taken longer than anticipated. She needed to wrap up her conversation ASAP so she and Sam could be on their way.

"How positive are you, Nancy, that our Hampton artist is the same forger you ran across in England four years ago?" Nancy Chester, a longtime advisor to MI-6 in art related forgeries and presently one of the current curators for the National Gallery in London, was on the other end of the line.

"One hundred percent. That photo you faxed me late last night confirmed everything. I've got to hand it to you, you've a knack for putting the pieces of a puzzle together quickly." The older woman's British accent came through crisp and clear. "I wondered if he'd ever surface again. Perhaps, somewhere on the continent, if he ever thought of doing so. I can't fathom why he thought he could go undetected in your area of all places. And for three years? Boggles my bloody mind, it does. He's in on this, luv. Mark my words."

"I know. The man's played the role of a hermit quite well, bringing out his artwork to sell by using a third party. Honest to God, I never suspected a thing either until late yesterday afternoon when I compared a few pictures I'd found on Google. Remember, I was with you when they arrested him after the Derbyshire affair. I'm so mad I didn't catch this. How the hell did he get out of jail?"

"Listen, I'll look into all that and get answers. But you have to tell the Director what you and I suspect. Promise me you'll be careful." Nancy's voice softened into a motherly tone much as the Director's had done on several occasions over the last few days. "And, not to change the subject. If you need a place to stay given the rumor you're leaving the Agency, come across the pond. I've bought a nice little cottage up in the Cotswolds. Perfect for being isolated. And great for rest and relaxation. Very friendly village, too."

Sarah was shocked her plan had traveled outside her inner circle. How had the woman found out? Trying to keep an upbeat tempo in her voice, she said, "Boy, that's definitely tempting. I'll be in touch. Remember to call my personal cell when you've dug into the heist a bit more. I'm running out of time."

"You go tend to what's needed. I'll call even though we're six hours apart. Just get the bloody bastard and his accomplice. I'd like the good old boys' network here to still know I'm good for something."

"I'll see the Director gives you some kind of recognition."

"Oh, and Sarah, don't let Sam have a heart attack when he sees you know who."

Sarah smiled, knowing to whom Nancy referred. She chuckled at their shared joke. "Got to go."

Her English friend replied, "Right. Be wary and stay safe." Click.

Sarah had no doubt the woman would be on her way to the MI6 office to look into paperwork of the heist the minute she hung up. Nancy would have answers within a few hours and could tell the Director who'd be taken into custody at the fundraiser. With the confirmation, the agents would move in. But there was still the unanswered question of where the stolen paintings were located. Maybe she and Sam would find the last clue after they made the short side trip to the Auction House that afternoon. Luck had to be on her side. She wanted to be away from Rick and well out of town come morning.

* * *

Easthampton Auction House

The day had finally arrived. After an intensive week of planning, briefings, plus a few unwanted society teas given in honor of her marriage to Rick, Sarah had had quite enough. She was raring to get things moving, especially having talked to Nancy earlier. Time to put her last mission front and center. If she had to be honest, she was going to miss the thrill of the hunt. But now, she couldn't only do for herself. There were two people to consider – her and her baby.

Sam Tanner was given the task to drive her to the Auction House. Their intent was to scope out the facility, make sure all was in place for the event of the night, and verify the intelligence received over the last few days.

Stopped in traffic, she could feel his eyes on her. Pivoting to look at her mentor, she returned his gaze. There definitely was something on his mind and she wasn't going to be able to evade the interrogation headed her way in the closed quarters of the car.

Clearing his throat, the deep tenor in his voice rang out, "You mentioned how your grandparents took your news. It couldn't have been easy to have that kind of conversation over the phone."

Sarah sighed and turned her head to glance out the passenger window. Given the choice, she'd much rather not share her private chat. However, thinking back on the times the man by her side had had her back, she knew she could confide in him.

"You can only imagine how Gram took everything. You've known her and Pop for years." Crossing her arms over her chest, she turned back and leveled a defiant look in his direction. "I can't believe the Director, who speaks of family always coming first, wouldn't let me go see them. That was really, really cruel, Sam. I'll never forgive her." Sarah paused and inhaled a deep breath in an attempt to calm and steady her nervous stomach. "If this wasn't my last assignment, it would be on that very issue alone." Tears welled up in her eyes as she thought of the emotional conversation with her grandmother. Not having a tissue handy, she swiped at her eyes with her blazer.

"What did she have to say?" Sam queried. "That is if you want to share."

Sarah couldn't be mad at the man's persistence. He'd stood in her corner when she and the Director had come to blows over the matter.

"Gram sounded happy." Sarah scrambled to convey the right words. "Deep down though, I sensed she was devastated and didn't want to let on. Gram's very religious. That old-fashioned Episcopalian guilt ate away at my gut. I was brought up in the church's way of things – you meet Mr. Right, you marry Mr. Right, and then, and only then, do have his baby. Look at me! Due to one foolish night, I've done everything ass backwards and let down the two people I love most." A lump formed in her throat. "And on top of everything, Gram announced there was no way she and Pop were up and leaving their friends in Hampton Beach! She stated they were born in Hampton Beach and would die there. Now, I've to rethink everything! When, pray tell, am I going to have time to do that while I'm in the middle of all this?" She looked at Sam who merely sat with his hands on the steering wheel. The man stared back, fatherly concern etched on his face. "Don't look at me like that, Sam Tanner."

"Like what?"

"You and the Director don't have secrets. I've no doubt the two of you discussed me in much greater detail." Sarah pointed at her belly.

The car began to inch forward, slowly making its way to the stop sign at Main Street.

"Sarah." The way Sam spoke to her was oddly comforting. But she wasn't prepared for what came next. "You *must* tell Rick about this baby. The man's got a right to be in his child's life." He paused. Sarah could tell he was mulling over something really important he had to impart. She couldn't help but lock her eyes with his. "If it were me, I'd certainly want to know if I were in his shoes."

Sarah adamantly shook her head from side to side. "No! No way! I'll be the only parent making the decisions for this baby I'm carrying. I know you mean well, but I've had enough from the Eagle on the subject, thank you very much."

"Sarah Ann Adams! Rick's simply not going..."

A horn honked from behind, their signal to move. Sam turned out onto Main Street, making his way to the Auction House that was located several blocks down the road.

Sarah glanced at her secure phone she held in her hand and scanned the screen. No coded messages from Command Central. That was a good sign. All was good to go. As Sam turned into the parking lot of the Auction House, Sarah rifled through the glove compartment.

"Sam, I can't find our preview passes." Then, she slammed the compartment shut and rummaged through her handbag, her anxiety growing. "Damn, we're not going to be able to get in without them."

Sam tapped the side pocket of his coat. "Right here, Sarah. Safe and sound. Lizzie slipped them to me on our way out the door. I should have told you." With the car parked, he shut off the engine. "Answer me this. Why isn't Rick here? Why me? Seems to me since you both are the 'buyers' tonight, he'd want to preview the goods and be seen."

"He didn't have a choice. Rick had to stay back at the house with his IT team for some reason. Plus, there's a conference call coming in from Scotland Yard, including the Director. Something dealing with information Rick found that bears on the warrants needed for the arrests tonight." Thinking back on her conversation with Nancy, she asked, "Sam, is it true the agent who said his paintings were stolen had a security system that rivaled Buckingham Palace?"

"Yup. That's why everyone doesn't believe his report to be true. And since we know his paintings are somewhere nearby, every avenue has been explored. I've known the agent from way back. Charles Brogan's an arrogant bastard. Just think of it. Charles walked on to a British Airways plane with a public manifest, waltzed into the Hamptons and showed up at a friend's estate. Red flags went up documenting his every move since he landed at JFK." Sam shook his head and stared over at her. "I still can't get over the fact he didn't think he'd be trailed."

Putting together what she'd learned from Nancy and her briefings, Sarah leaned back in her seat to contemplate the relationship of the stolen artwork and an artist who could forge a painting.

Sam jarred her from her musings. "How long do you plan on sitting here? Those passes are only good for a brief window of time. To be honest, I'm a bit nervous, even with all the agents present. Tell me you're armed."

Sarah tapped her left boot. "Right here, boss. My small caliber pistol." Seeing another troubled look cross Sam's face, she smiled warmly to assuage his fear, poking him in the shoulder. "How many times have we worked these ops? Relax."

"This time I've every right to be overly cautious. You have that baby," Sam pointed to her stomach. "I couldn't live with myself should you get hurt."

"I'm fine. I'd say so if I wasn't." She tapped his knee to reassure him. "I'll be extra careful. Tonight, though, is a whole different ball game."

"Then we better get a move on. Let's go see what's waiting for us behind those doors."

"I'm with you." Sarah replied and opened the car door to get out. "Let's go." *I only hope you don't blow when you see who's waiting inside.*

CHAPTER THIRTEEN

Sam and Sarah walked up the steps to the entrance of the Easthampton Auction House. Having shown their passes to the two guards at the front door, they were admitted and faced a second round of screening as they passed through the grand foyer and approached the French doors that led to the main ballroom where the fundraiser would be held that night. Sarah breathed a sigh of relief seeing Agency guards dressed incognito as members of the Easthampton Police Department. Check one item off her list.

A hushed voice resonated in her ear. "I've got your back. You just do your thing. I'll follow your cue. Signal me when it's time to go."

The agent at the left French door opened it and motioned for Sam and her to enter.

"Copy that." Sarah locked her arm through the crook of his elbow and walked into the large room impressively decked out for the night's festivities. Her gaze felt on the stage and she halted dead in her tracks.

"What's wrong?" Sam piped up beside her.

"At every preview I've ever been to the paintings are roped off at the front of the room for the public to view before the auction. Look. Nothing's there." She pointed to the cordoned off area. "I didn't receive anything that said old MacDennis had backed out on selling his artwork. There was quite a write up in yesterday's ***Hampton Times***. What do you know about him?"

"The hermit? Hardly anything, quite frankly. Don't normally keep an eye on the coming and goings in the Hamptons. That's why we've got you. But there's something amiss, don't you think?"

"What?" Sarah's eyes darted in every direction, her brain scrambling to think why everything was not as it should be.

"I was just wondering where the curator is. You know the one Lizzie said was going to meet us."

Sarah quickly replied, "Ah, yes." *Oh boy, he's going to blow.* "I've been meaning to..."

Heavy footsteps were heard coming up from behind them.

"You must be Sarah Stockton that my Lizzie raves about!" A masculine voice with a heavy Scottish accent called out.

She and Sam did an about face.

"Bloody hell! What are you doing here of all places?" Sam was non-too pleased. Sarah had warned the Director that Sam should be informed his former partner was in on the operation from the other side of the pond. Especially since the two had parted company and never remained in touch. Something had happened. What that was, Sarah had no idea. The Director, when probed, remained mute on the subject.

Stepping between the two men, Sarah said, "Sir Oswald! It's so nice to finally get a chance to meet you in person. The Director gives you high marks." Her mentor grumbled beside her. "But, I thought we wouldn't be meeting you until tonight."

"A slight change in plans my dear." His eyes lit on Sam. "Well, well. Samuel Tanner. I can't believe it's you."

Was it her imagination, but was Sir Oswald taunting Sam?

Sam stood ramrod straight, hands clenched at his sides. "What brings you to the States? The last I heard you were happily retired and enjoying your life in Edinburg. Sarah, did you know Sir Oswald and I go way back..." the man cleared his throat, then added, "to the days when gentlemen were gentlemen."

Oh boy. What had gone down between these two? Sarah slightly nudged Sam in the ribs, giving him a "behave yourself" look out of the corner of her eye. She hoped it would be enough for him to remember he had a role to play. The two men could have a pissing match later. She'd a mission to get done today and one final report to make.

"Well, it's very nice to meet you, Sir Oswald." She shook hands with the gentleman, however he made her a bit uncomfortable when he held onto hers a bit longer than necessary.

"And I you, lass. Congratulations are in order I hear."

"Enough with the how-do-you dos!" Sam barked. "We're supposed to be meeting a curator to preview the paintings. I don't see anyone."

Sam's old partner grinned and nodded his head toward the staging area. He motioned for Sam and her to follow him. "I've been given that honor. With what we now know, the Director made a decision to keep the hermit's paintings up in the wings. There are cameras hidden all over, and agents, too. One can't be too careful when dealing with Charles Brogan."

As they reached the stairs to go up and into the wings, Sam asked, "And you'd know this how?"

"We both know how arrogant a bastard he can be, Sam. We saw it ourselves many years ago. I've come out of retirement to put the bloody bastard in jail once and for all. And to settle a few other cases I still believe he got away with."

Sarah watched, fascinated, as the two men seemed to have set their differences aside for the good of the cause. She prayed they'd continue, but her curiosity was piqued.

Once in the wings, Sir Oswald swiped a security card through a metal box and two doors swung open. A private vault. Wow, something's up if the auction is being this cautious, she thought. Within the large room, set up on easels, were the paintings of "the hermit", each labeled with its title that matched the picture brochure she'd picked up in the lobby.

Constrained by time to try and determine why these particular paintings might have anything to do with the stolen art, she asked, "Would it be possible for me to take a really close look?"

"By all means. Look away. I'm not a pro at this, but there's some connection. I have to admit, having been to the Hamptons myself just a few times, he really captured the beauty of the local landscapes. While you're busy, Sam and I will catch up. I hear you're the art expert. Take a really good look."

Had Sir Oswald actually winked or was there a tic she should have picked up on?

Acting on the man's invitation, Sarah moved from one painting to the other, comparing them to the brochure she'd taken out from her handbag. It was the fourth painting that made her pause. Staring at it from every angle, the landscape did not seem to come across as it had in the brochure's photo. Sure, it seemed to look as if it were real, but her training in art classes told her something was askew. And then, the light bulb went off. Looking back over her shoulder, she saw Sam and his former partner deep in a private discussion…a peaceful talk, thank goodness.

From her pocket, she withdrew a mini-lens wrapped in tissue and began to scrutinize the painting from corner to corner. It was the dark clouds in the picture where she finally saw the last clue. The picture was of a stormy day, the clouds dark and ominous. The sea curled with heavy surf and foaming water rushed up and onto the sand.

Sarah carefully noted the brush stokes, especially in the top left hand corner where the black cloud was strategically placed. She urgently needed to remove a small layer of the black paint. She was positive something lay beneath. What she attempted to do could ruin the painting to the naked eye, but she'd come prepared.

Restoration was her favorite class at GW, and she'd actually learned a few tricks from Nancy while she'd been in London. Taking a deep breath to steady her shaky hand, she flecked her fingernail across the small mound of thick paint. It came flying off, settling in the tissue she held in her hand, a few smaller pieces landing at her feet. There behind the hermit's work of "art" was another color…and another painting! Sarah gasped out loud.

"Something wrong, Sarah?" Sam's tone seemed to warn her to be wary.

She dared not turn around. "No. Nothing. This particular one took me by surprise. I'm sure it's of Jetty Four. Rick has to bid on this one tonight. I won't be much longer. I promise."

"Lizzie said to take your time, luv." The Scotsman's thick brogue shared the same concern as Sam moments earlier.

"I'm almost done." She took a charcoal pencil from her right-hand pocket and penciled over the damaged surface. Stepping back, she studied her work. No one would notice. Finally, she had the answer to what they'd needed. The Director and all agencies involved could make their move. She had to get back to Thomas's house. Satisfied she'd covered up the dark spot, she turned and walked over to the two men.

Sarah tugged at her ear as she approached the two and Sam shook the hand of his former partner.

"Well, looks like we'll be off. Will you be here tonight, Sir Oswald?" Sarah was curious. She didn't know the man. And she'd had her share of dealing with double agents.

"Yes. Wouldn't miss it for the world." Sir Oswald grinned. "It's been a pleasure meeting you. I know you'll be busy tonight." Motioning to a different door in the wings, he said, "After you." This time, he typed a code into a key pad that closed the doors behind them as they exited the area. Escorting them to the main entrance, he bowed at the waist. "I'll see you this evening."

Back in the SUV, Sam turned to stare at her. "Come on. Give. You tugged your ear. Something's afoot. Out with it. What is it?"

"You didn't seem to like Sir Oswald. Do you trust him?" Sarah bombarded Sam with questions regarding his relationship with the Scottish gentleman. Some Sam answered. Others, he remained silent.

"We had a parting of the ways over an issue a long time ago. But, yes, if push came to shove, I'd trust him with my life. However, you seem to be evading my questions. What happened in there?"

Finally, at the car, the two climbed in. Sam started the engine.

"All I'll say is we've got a lot to change before tonight. The paintings up for sale are painted over the stolen ones. Nice, huh?"

Sarah watched as a stunned look came over Sam's face. She'd barely buckled herself into her seat when Sam pushed on the gas pedal a bit too hard. Their car shot forward, narrowly missing a black Porsche parked by the sidewalk adjacent to the Auction House. Neither Sam nor Sarah saw Sir Oswald get into the passenger side of the car. Had they looked carefully enough, Sir Oswald had a companion – one with a bald head and a closely cropped salt and pepper beard. A man who went by the name of Charles Brogan.

CHAPTER FOURTEEN

Auction House Fundraiser

Rick couldn't take his eyes off Sarah as she walked down the grand staircase of his Easthampton home. She wore the blue sequined ball gown, the dress that took his breath away the night of the infamous wedding. Only, now, she glowed. There was something different about the way she held herself, how she filled out the dress. Earlier, he'd heard her arguing with the Director about some sort of "fit" and "Stop playing with my hair and makeup. I look just fine." He considered himself a lucky man. Or would be, come the conclusion of the night when he would finally make things right. It was his intent to get down on one knee and make the proposal he spent all day rehearsing. His heart burst with love for the woman. He wanted her mind, body, and soul for the rest of his life. Then, for real, Sarah could start planning the wedding of her dreams.

Waiting for her at the bottom of the staircase, he watched her descend, her eyes never leaving the band of sapphires and diamonds he placed on her ring finger the night they arrived. She told him time and again, during their stay at his estate, "I'm wearing it for appearance sake!" But Rick was heartened to know she loved what he picked out.

Reaching out to take hold of her hand as she reached the last step, he was surprised she didn't shy away. How could a man be so fortunate, and then throw it all away in one night? If luck was on his side, the woman would be glowing by morning and he'd make sure she would continue to do so every morning thereafter.

Deep in thought, Rick realized Sarah was tugging on his tuxedo jacket. He eyed the waiting crowd to find all eyes trained on him.

"Well, are you coming, or are you just going to stand there and gape at your 'wife' all night? Remember there's a job to be done, Richard. The sooner it's accomplished, the better." Elizabeth Hallock's voice rang out as if she were ordering her troops into battle.

Hell, he was nervous. From personal experience he knew what could go wrong. His sister was practically blown to kingdom come during her last mission, but this time it was his Sarah in the line of fire. He prayed all day long something would come up needing her attention and force her to stay behind tonight. Safe. But, that hadn't happened. She was an agent for the CIA, with a job to do, and he had to accept that fact whether he liked it or not.

"Let's go, Romeo." Another tug on his sleeve made him look deep into the eyes of the woman standing beside him. "You and I have a ruse to play. The Director's team will take things from there. The limo is waiting, Rick. I'll let you in on a little secret. The Director wasn't happy with our hurried briefing and the quick changes we had to make tonight work."

Rick was curious. "What do mean?" "You'll find out in due time. That's all I'll tell you. I don't want her more miffed than she already is." Sarah dragged him down the hallway and out the front door.

Climbing into the stretch limo, Rick realized Sam and the Director had decided to join them for the ride. To calm his nerves, he reached for Sarah's hand, but she attempted to pull away. "Hey," he said. "You just told me to play the part. I'm practicing." A soft snicker of laughter echoed from the opposite side of the limo.

"Just stick to the plan," Sarah retorted.

"Yes, ma'am." Rick squeezed her fingers a bit harder.

It took longer than anticipated to reach the Auction House. Traffic was backed up in every direction. Limousines and Town Cars could be seen everywhere. In the Hamptons it was all about making "the entrance".

"Operation Painting Party underway." Elizabeth's voice transmitted into the diamond pin she wore on her dress. The broach was a mini-microphone which would aid in her ability to stay in touch with her agents as well as the earpiece worn in her right ear. "Copy that, Agent McVey. Over."

Knowing Sarah was equally equipped with a plug as well, Rick and his "wife" were to keep the bidding moving and report on anything out of the ordinary. Now closing in on the venue and having to be ready to play the role of a lifetime, he felt as if his bow tie was strangling him. Sticking his finger up between his white shirt and the tie, he managed to loosen it a bit. Nerves, he thought. *You're not normally "on* the *ground" so to speak.*

"Relax, darling," Sarah let out a dream-like sigh. For Rick it would be the perfect night if sometime during the evening she countered she loved him in return. "Look. We're here. Put on your best 'I love you look' and let's do this up right!"

Security was tight. Once inside, Elizabeth made prearrangements for the trio to retrieve their weapons. When the Director announced she and Sarah needed to use the ladies' room, Sam came to stand by Rick's side.

"Sarah's one fine looking woman. Don't you go messing with my girl, Rick. You copy that?"

"Yes, sir." Rick looked eye to eye with one of Sarah's biggest advocates.

"You'll answer to me, boy. You understand? She is leaving the Agency as you well know, but..."

"Say what?" A bomb exploded within his heart. What the hell had Sam meant?

"All set." The ladies were back. Sarah tapped her thigh, smiling at him, a sly grin on her face. "Ready for action, Romeo?"

Oh, I'm ready for some action. Just the mere gesture of her tapping her thigh gave him a hard on. Picturing the gun she wore under her dress, touching her long tanned legs that wrapped around him mere months ago, made all the blood in his body rush to his groin.

Moving into the grand arena, a waiter came forward with champagne. Rick chose two glasses, but Sarah shied away when he offered her one of the two flutes.

"No, thanks. Ginger ale for me, Rick. I'm on the job."

However, the Director and Sam gladly took the offered bubbly beverage and fell into a deep conversation with the hosts of the event: Samantha and Steven Barrington. Rick passed off the unwanted glass to a passing waiter, took Sarah's hand in his, and strolled over to join the group. Rick had been delegated one major job – keep his eyes on one person in particular. Agent Sarah Adams. He intended to do just that.

* * *

Come on. Get the show on the road. Sarah grew restless moving from one area of the room to the other with Rick by her side. If one more person offered congratulations, she thought she'd barf. Actually, when she really had a moment to stop and think, without the mission reeling through her mind, she realized she wasn't feeling quite well, and hadn't since earlier that morning. Had she mentioned that fact to the Director, she'd be sitting back at 1450 Bishop Lane, watching things play out from Command Central. Maybe it was the swell of the crowd, the heat in the room was stifling.

"Ladies and gentlemen. Please take your seats. All the numbers for the bidding have been given out." The auctioneer's voice came over the PA system.

People rapidly pushed and shoved to get the best seats. It was then she realized Rick had left her alone. Could the man not do one simple job? Was he not supposed to be watching her? With a brief scan of the room, she spotted him, sitting in the first row, front and center. He waved his hand, holding three fingers in the air. Knowing the Director would never deliberately draw attention to herself on a mission, Sarah put up one finger. Rick understood the need for one seat, nodding in return. As she made her way through the crowd, she was suddenly stunned by the thought of how she could walk away from a man who respected her for what she did, went to the lengths to make her job work, and, above all, respected her. She'd come to realize over the last several days maybe she erred in her thinking as she lived with him in such close quarters. But could a leopard change his spots? Was it possible he could love her?

Immediately, she admonished herself. *Remember his reputation! You're the one who's knocked up! You fell for his 'I've never felt like this with anyone else before' line. It's over. You're moving on. After tonight, he's going to be gone from your life. Isn't that what you wanted and planned for?*

Just as she made her way to the front row, someone pulled at her arm and spun her around. Sir Oswald!

"Mrs. Stockton! Such a pleasure to see you again! I say you're looking quite ravishing this evening. That must your handsome husband I take it?" Sir Oswald pointed at Rick. "Forgive me. But may I inquire as to why didn't you explore the art arena after you left George Washington? Why ever did you settle and become a manager of a beach club?"

The man certainly knew a lot about her. Was it all part of the ruse, the roles they were all to play? She let him ramble on. "I wanted to tell you you're correct in bidding on painting number four. It was done at Jetty Four. Or so says old Mac Dennis. Crusty old man. Don't like him one bit. You?"

It dawned on her he, too, was in the possession of classified information known only to five people. No one knew, other than the people who'd attended the briefing at Rick's estate, the stolen paintings were in fact in full view of the audience. Only a select few were in on the classified information needed to close the sting tonight.

The Scotsman started to fidget in front of her, a devilish twinkle played in his eyes. "I must go. Really, really, enjoy, Sarah. I hope you get the painting you came for."

Again - the wink. Just like the one he'd sent her way that afternoon as he strolled away. Sarah kept her eyes glued on him. The man didn't take his seat near the front as she thought he would, instead he walked to the back row. He took a seat next to a tall, bearded man. Stunned, she couldn't believe who she saw – Charles Brogan! As her heart rapidly pounded in her chest, out of the corner of her eye she spied Sam and a few "EPD" agents change their positions. Good. Close the ranks and make a smaller perimeter to monitor.

Having reached her seat, Rick leaned in and whispered, "Who was that guy? You look as if you've seen a ghost. The man certainly wanted to bend your ear about something."

Not thinking what placing her hand on his arm might imply, Rick covered it with his own, squeezing tight. All she could do was glance up at him and smile, hoping he'd stop with the questions, professionally related or otherwise. "Oh, he's just an old friend of the Director and Sam." She needed Rick back on track regarding his role. "Just remember when we get to painting four, I'll nudge you and say I'm sick. You're going to stand up and..."

"Don't worry. The Director was very explicit on my instructions."

Sarah cringed as his voice rang out. She leaned towards him. "Lower your voice!"

"Arguing already? Aren't you two supposed to be on your honeymoon?"

Sarah pivoted in her seat, hearing the familiar voice of Courtney Hallock. Accompanied by her husband, Thomas, the woman wore a sly grin on her face. Sarah was now mad at herself for spending far too long rationalizing her feelings for Rick. She should have had her mind on Sir Oswald's behavior.

"You've heard the news?" Courtney tapped her right ear. She, too, had an earpiece.

With her mind reeling with who, what, where and when, she'd not kept track of the chatter. "What news?" She eyed her friend curiously.

"Well, I don't have to tell you, of all people, the paintings are secure." Courtney nodded towards the stage. "Old MacDennis was picked up an hour ago at Gabreski. There was a manifest filed for a flight tonight. The FBI surrounded the jet and nabbed him. Brogan's going to be taken into custody once the auction starts. Sir Oswald's been given that honor. Brogan actually used his friend's wife to help hide the paintings at their estate on Gin Lane. She tripped the alarm system when they loaded up the paintings early yesterday morning for the delivery here to the Auction House. Apparently, the guy was thinking with his you know what and not with his brain." Courtney chuckled and shook her head. "Can you believe it?"

Immediately the puzzle pieces clicked together. Sir Oswald was confirming that the paintings were right under her nose just as she'd discovered.

The auctioneer came to the podium. "Ladies and gentlemen, paddles at the ready."

"Let's talk later, Court." Sarah turned back to her bird's eye view of the stage. As she did so, a sudden pain started in her lower back and shot down her leg. *Damn these shoes! I wanted to wear pumps. But oh no. I had to have the shoes that went with the dress that reminded me of him. Stupid!*

"May we have the first painting up for sale?" The auctioneer was well known in the Hamptons, especially having worked for many years at Sotheby's in New York City. Two men lifted a large, rectangular shaped painting onto the easel nearby. *Montauk in Winter* read the program.

Sarah now completely understood why the Director had insisted, to Samantha Barrington's consternation, that she be in control of the guest list. Renown artists weren't invited for the simple reason of telling a real painting from a forgery and putting their sting in jeopardy.

Sarah nudged Rick in his side. "Bid two hundred thousand."

Rick held up his paddle and called out the amount.

"Two hundred thousand from number 36. Do I hear four?"

From across the room, a shout for four hundred thousand was heard, then six, then eight, then, one million. Finally, the auctioneer cried out, "Sold to the gentleman with paddle number 42."

Sarah swiveled her head around curious as to who'd won the first painting. Much to her surprise, Sir Oswald held the paddle number marked number forty-two. Turning in her direction, he gave her a "thumbs up". It dawned on Sarah it was the Director's plan to keep the auction moving at a "normal" pace, for the time being, while keeping the paintings in the hands of her agents.

With all the chattering in the room around her, the next item didn't come up for bid immediately. Sarah went to stand and stretch, but suddenly realized she couldn't. Something was wrong. Out of nowhere a searing, hot pain shot through her belly, settling in her midsection. *No! Not my baby*!

"Rick! Rick!" Sarah shook the edge of his jacket in an attempt to grab hold of his attention. He was standing, as were others around them, his eyes glued to the commotion coming from the other side of the room. "Rick! Please!" She was suddenly short of breath. "I'm going to be…"

"Not now." Rick brushed her hand away, not looking down to see her distress. "The Director said to wait until…" How was she going to get his attention? Giving his pants a hard tug, and pinching his thigh, he finally turned and glanced down. His eyes widened in horror, realizing her anguished state. He quickly knelt down, flinging his arms around her. "Sarah! Sarah! Oh, my God! Courtney, go get help!" he yelled to the woman behind them. "See if you can find a doctor!"

Barely conscious, Sarah felt Rick put his arms about her. He picked her up, cradling her to his chest as they sat waiting for medical attention to arrive.

Why, why can't I just admit it? He's the love of my life. My love. And I want a life…with only him. With him, I'll always be home.

Then the darkness claimed her once more.

CHAPTER FIFTEEN

Southampton Hospital

Rick couldn't sit in the hard chair any longer. For five hours, he'd been closeted with Sam Tanner and members of the Hallock family in the private conference room outside the ICU. He rose, stretched his stiff body, and walked to the open door.

Slamming his hand in frustration against the door frame, Sam came to stand beside him. "Now we don't need to be taking you down to the E.R. with a broken wrist. I know this is tough, but news will come soon."

"I can't believe we haven't been given anything more definitive." He pointed to the clock on the wall. "Look what time it is."

"That's the HIPAA regulations," Sam replied. "The reason Elizabeth isn't here doesn't have anything to do with the cleanup of the Operation Painting Party. She had two of her body guards chopper her to Hampton Beach. She's breaking the news to Sarah's grandmother. Then, she'll bring Gram to the hospital as she is the only one, besides Elizabeth, who can have medical access to what's going on with Sarah behind those green doors." Sam's arm came around Rick's shoulders. "You look as if you could use the coffee the staff graciously provided. How about I get you a cup?"

Rick turned from the doorway and glanced back into the room, seeing the worried expressions on everyone's faces. Sarah was family to all who sat there quietly: Courtney, Thomas, Matt, Megan, Helen and Robert. "Thanks. I'd appreciate that. I really need to get something to eat. We never got a chance last night..." His voice trailed off, his mind thinking of holding Sarah's limp, unconscious body in his arms.

"How about I get you a sandwich from the cafeteria, Rick? You'll get much better nourishment than those doughnuts over there." Shelby had snuck up behind the two men. When everything went down last night, Matt had the foresight to call her. After all, she was Sarah's best friend. Matt said she'd want to be with them, but would also serve a useful purpose in case the family needed help translating anything medical that might get thrown their way into layman's terms.

"Shelby," Rick replied, trying hard to put a smile on his face. "I was engrossed thinking about Sarah I didn't see you come in. I'm really glad you're here."

Shelby's voice cracked when she replied, "I wouldn't choose to be anywhere else. That's my best friend in there. What kind of sandwich...?" The chatter coming from the doorway made her stop.

Through the door walked the Director accompanied by Sarah's grandmother, who sat in a wheelchair, pushed by Doc

Davis. No one in the room said a word. They patiently waited for one of the three to speak.

Doc Davis spoke up first. "Since I'm Sarah's primary care doctor and I've already been on the phone with big wigs here, I think it best that I go in first. I'll be able to get an up to date status on our girl. Then, Gram," he got down on one knee beside her wheelchair and raised his voice so she could hear him, "the doctor will want to see you and Elizabeth. I explained almost everything on the ride over."

The elderly woman's hands trembled as she held her quilted handbag in her lap. Her voice shook. "Sounds like a fine plan, Doc. Go in and find out how my Sarah's doing. Go on now."

Doc gave her shoulder a reassuring squeeze. "I'll be back as soon as I can."

Viewing the interchange, Rick was stunned, having never met Sarah's grandmother. How alike Sarah and the elderly woman were in their mannerisms. It was as if he was seeing the woman he loved sixty years into the future.

Gram surveyed the people in the room. "Lizzie, push me in a bit farther. I want to see everyone clearly. These glasses aren't too great." The Director did as requested. Once the Director had locked the wheels on her wheelchair, Gram spoke. "I want to thank all of you for being here. I know how much you love my Sarah. Believe me, she returns your love twofold. And you..." The elderly woman's arthritic finger pointed at Rick. "You have a lot to answer for." A collective gasp was heard around the room.

Rick reached for the nearest chair and sat down, stunned. Did her grandmother know about the night they'd spent together? Was she upset for him not acting more gentlemanly and do the honorable thing? So engrossed in his own thoughts, he didn't see the Director and Gram leave the private room.

Shelby came again to sit by him. She tapped him on his knee, bringing him out of his musings. "Sarah's tough, Rick. She'll be okay. But you have to make me a promise."

Still rattled, Rick asked, "And what would that be?"

"Promise me you'll listen to Sarah. You have to hear her out. Don't condemn her or be angry. Let her tell you everything. You hear me, Rick? She has suffered too much on her own already."

Shelby was scaring him. What exactly was she referring to? Shaking his head, he tried to make sense of Shelby's ramblings. It was if the woman was talking in riddles.

The conference room became eerily quiet. Rick noticed everyone's eyes were trained on the door where a nurse, dressed in blue scrubs and holding a clipboard, now stood. "I need Rick Stockton. Is he here?"

Realizing his legs were shaking he stood up. "That would be me."

"Come." The woman commanded.

"Where are you taking me?"

To see Sarah and her…oh, how shall I refer to them? Bodyguards?" The nurse laughed out loud. "You better hope you have your Wonder Boy underwear on today, hotshot."

* * *

It was inevitable after having talked with Gram that Rick wouldn't be far behind. Her grandmother sat patiently by her bedside. She clasped Sarah's hand in her wrinkled one as she listened to the multitude of doctors come and give their reports. Finding out Sarah would be fine, her grandmother's main focus was on the health of her unborn great-grand-child, who thankfully came through the ordeal unscathed. However, Sarah wasn't happy about the fact she'd have to spend the next two weeks in the hospital monitored and on total bed rest. Then, she could return to her apartment, still on limited bed rest, with 24/7 care around the clock. The only thing that made the final two weeks of downtime palat-able was Doc had granted Shelby a month's leave from the clinic to see to her. Her best friend would be bunking with Sarah for the duration. Sarah attempted to speak as the doc-tors conferred with the Director and Gram but was ignored.

Feeling her blood pressure rise from the stress of all she'd been through, and knowing it wasn't good for the baby, she decided to screw being the perfect patient. She pleaded, "May I say something? You're all talking as if I'm not in the room."

"Would you like Doc and I to leave, Sarah?" The Director asked.

"No. I just want to get some things off my chest. Everyone in here is family. Please just hear me out." She turned to face her grandmother and squeezed the hand of the woman who'd always been there for her. "Gram, I've wanted to tell you ev-ery minute detail. I'm wracked with guilt for not doing so when I had the chance. After we talked, I thought you were so disappointed in me. I should have come to you and told you everything when Doc confirmed I was pregnant and should have sought your guidance from that day on. If I had, maybe I wouldn't be in this...mess." Her eyes fell on the Director, taking in her red eyes. Why, the woman had been crying!

"Oh, Sarah," Elizabeth interjected, "I never should have insisted you do this one last assignment, especially once I knew about your condition. This is all my fault for putting stress on you and that baby." Sarah watched her boss take a tissue from her pocket and wipe at her eyes. "You insisted you had to take time off per Doc's orders. I was so selfish by not listening to either Doc or you. I needed you for one last job...with Rick."

Sarah was about to reply, but Gram beat her to the punch. "Elizabeth, you and I both know Sarah. If she agrees to do something, she's too professional to not see the job to the end." Her grandmother turned back and looked Sarah up and down one more time. "Honey, how do you plan on raising this baby? You mentioned you were going to move away. How can you do that, child? Honey, you're going to need your family and friends for support, dear."

Sarah didn't want to have this particular discussion at that moment. Given that only Elizabeth and Doc were the only others in the room, she stated, "I'm going to raise the baby myself." Sarah placed a loving hand on her slightly bulging belly. "I guess I'm going to have to rethink things a bit more because I want you and Pop to play an important role in its life. Without the demands of the Agency or the beach club, I'll finally have the time to take care of all of us. We can all be together. I have plenty of money."

"Stop right there, Sarah Ann Adams." Sarah couldn't remember the last time her grandmother used such a sharp tone with her. "If you're thinking of moving away from Hampton Beach, I told you Pop and I are very happy where we are. I'm putting my foot down. You're not leaving town, young lady. Not with my great-grand baby. Understood?"

Too tired to argue, Sarah could only shake her head in the affirmative. Sarah's voice cracked. "But how do I raise my baby in such a small town? Rick can't know about this baby. I am going to..."

"There is no way in hell you are going to take my baby off to live God knows where!" Rick stood just inside the door. His arms were crossed over his wrinkled shirt; his eyes blood shot. It had been hours since he slept. His body language registered defiance and the tone in his voice told her he was taking charge. "For the record, I've *every* intention of helping raise our child. Our baby is going to have a wonderful life, full of joy and laughter, and receive loving attention from *both* its parents. And to be clear, you, Sarah, are not leaving Hampton Beach. Period."

"Who's going to stop me?" The monitor at the side of Sarah's bed started to make loud beeping noises.

"You better put an end to this, Richard." Elizabeth's stern voice left no doubt she was about to do the man bodily harm. "The doctor said no one is to get her upset."

As he moved from where he stood inside the doorway, he took one look at her boss and asked, "Is it in your pocket?"

Sarah watched as the Director nodded, reached into her pocket, and pulled out both the diamond ring he'd given her in the limo along with the diamond and sapphire wedding band.

Taking the engagement ring from the Director, placing it in the palm of his hand. He came and stood in front of her grandmother. "I wish Sarah's Pop could be here. I'd like to ask your blessing to marry your granddaughter. I've loved her from the day we met. There's no one like her, and there never will be. She'll want for nothing. I promise you."

Sarah's jaw sagged, watching as her grandmother beamed from ear to ear. "You're going to see to it she stays in Hampton Beach? I want my great-grandbaby in my life."

"I will. But, if it's okay with you, for now, I'll move her into my Easthampton home until I can find one that's closer to you and Pop."

"Well, if she doesn't say yes, I will." Gram laughed, her face lit up, her eyes twinkling in delight. "Come here. Give me a hug." Rick leaned over and accepted her loving embrace. "Pop and I give you our blessing, but you better ask my girl properly." She turned and winked at Sarah.

Sarah reached for the tissues at the side of her bed. Just seeing the interchange between her grandmother and the man she loved caused the waterworks to flow.

Her eyes followed Rick as he walked to the other side of her hospital bed. Kneeling down on one knee, he spoke softly, "Sarah Ann Adams, I love you more than life itself. I've always loved you. Will you make me the happiest man on earth and be my wife?" She looked down at the infamous diamond ring.

Bursting into tears, all Sarah could do was nod and hold out her left hand. Rick slid the ring onto her finger, bent over the bed and hugged her to him. He backed away, looked into her eyes, then kissed her deeply to seal the deal.

After getting her emotions under control, she replied, "I love you, too. Are you ready to take on a bride with a plus one?"

Sarah saw genuine excitement in Rick's eyes.

"Honey, I'm over the moon! When's he due?"

"He? Oh, no. It's going to be a she, Rick. A mini-me. And the baby is due sometime around the beginning of April. Right, Doc?" When Sarah tried to look behind Rick for confirmation, the room erupted in cheers. With her focus totally on Rick's proposal, the entire clan, rounded up by Sam, had gathered in the room to share in the big event.

"Don't ever let me go, Romeo." Happy tears streamed down her cheeks. This was the one time she didn't bother to wipe them away.

Rick sat down on the edge of her bed, his eyes only for her. "Never, Juliet. You've given me a new lease on life, Sarah. You've made me whole and complete." He brought her hand up to his lips, pressing a kiss on her palm.

"Oh! Tell me I can start planning a wedding!" A familiar voice called from within the crowd.

Sarah shook her head in disbelief. Helen Hallock. Her voice roared above the crowd and grabbed everyone's attention. "When's the big day going to be? Just let me get my calendar out of my purse."

Sarah leveled a look at Rick. The two were on the same wave-length.

"You might as well be the one to tell her." Rick said.

Sarah couldn't be happier. To the Hamptons' official wedding planner, she announced. "Go right ahead. But, Rick and I want to be married at St. Mark's at Christmas."

EPILOGUE

Christmas Eve

Reverend Wade had squawked when Helen Hallock informed him Rick and Sarah wanted to be married around Christmas, the most sacred of holidays other than Easter. When the two chose Christmas Eve as the day for their nuptials, the man almost had a heart attack. However, when the Hallock Foundation offered to fix all the stain glass windows, he made every effort to find a time during the twenty-fourth, normally filled with Christmas services, to marry the two.

With the ceremony over, it took a little bit of ingenuity on Shelby's part to configure Sarah and her dream bridal gown into the white Rolls Royce parked at the curb of St. Mark's Church. As predicted, the snow flurries had arrived. Rick climbed in the opposite door while Shelby shoved Sarah's bridal bouquet of Christmas greeneries into her hands.

"Tom and I are right behind you. We're riding with Rob."

Her maid of honor closed the door and the vintage Rolls Royce, in which they rode, took off down the long driveway.

"Everyone thinks we're nuts, you know." Rick's eyes filled with love and desire. "Are you sure you're up for this?" Picking up her right hand, he kissed it as a prince would his princess. "You're mine, Sarah Ann Adams Stockton. I'm never letting you go."

Sarah patted her belly. "It's me and Baby Stockton. Remember we're a package deal. And, FYI. I don't care if people think we're crazy. Rob says it's almost sunset at Jetty Four. There's just enough of a window of time to take a few pictures. You know how much I've loved our walks along the beach these last few months. I want a picture of us there, of all places, on our special day. And who better to take the photos?"

Rob was a well-known photographer in Hampton Beach, taking photos of the landscapes and beaches. His wife, who'd answered the phone the day Sarah called, was over the moon at the very thought her husband would take photographs for a Hampton society wedding. Over the past several months, she'd become fast friends with Sarah and Shelby, even getting invited into the circle of "girls' night out".

Rick shook his head, laughing as he did so. "You're crazy, but that's what I love about you. Thank goodness, the wind's died down. It's cold, plus the snow's falling."

On the ride to the beach, Sarah sat mesmerized by the dress she wore. It was everything she'd ever dreamed of. High necked, with capped sleeves, the dress was covered in Belgian lace. The lace was her "something old", having been stored and preserved for years in her grandmother's trunk. The dress was just what she ordered when Rick granted her wish of having it professionally designed. A mix of a Cinderella fairy tale with a contemporary flare. It molded to her ever-growing torso and Sarah didn't mind one bit. She was proud people knew she was having Rick's baby.

Since it was only a five-minute drive from the church to the beach, Rob had sent his helpers when the service ended to set up his equipment.

Climbing out of the Rolls was just as complicated as getting in.

"We're coming," she yelled up to Rob, who stood waving at the top of the landing.

"Hurry up! The light's perfect. I can only grab a few shots!" Rob shouted down at her entourage.

Finally making it to the top of the stairs, with Rick by her side, and Shelby and Tom in tow, Rob positioned them, first with the jetty and ocean behind them. Looking up into her husband's eyes and feeling his hand on their child, Sarah felt the true meaning of everlasting love. She nestled into his shoulder, hugging him to her, hearing the rapid click of Rob's camera in the background.

Rob commented, "Damn, it's cold! Now, turn so the bay's in the background. Same pose. Tom and Shelby? Jump into the last two shots." Cold as well, the wedding party did as instructed. "Perfect. Great pictures, if I do say so." Rob sounded pleased. Sarah couldn't wait to see the proofs. "Now get back in your car. The four of you must be frozen. At least I've got a coat."

Sarah lifted up the hem of her gown as she descended the staircase to the waiting Rolls Royce. Shelby once again helped her into the car, shut the door, then hurried to climb into the limo behind them.

Back in the warm car, Rick exclaimed, "We've a party to go to Mrs. Stockton!" The look in his eyes matched the one she'd seen when he saw her for the first time in her wedding gown. It was one of the moments that would be forever etched in her memory. She remembered gripping Sam Tanner's arm a bit tighter to steady her as they strolled down the red-carpeted aisle to where Rick waited along with Tom, Shelby and Reverend Wade. Gram and Pop stood in the front pew, holding hands, ready to say their part in giving her away.

Sarah couldn't contain her excitement. "We certainly do, husband! The night is young. Our families are waiting." She paused, her eyes twinkling with delight and mischief.

"What are you thinking about now, wife?"

"Only that tonight, my love, we're going to be sleeping in *our* bed."

THE END

Did you enjoy Christmas, Hamptons' Style? This book is part of a unique series known as ***Hampton Thoroughbreds*** – where romance meets action and adventure, and deceit lies just over the dunes. The books are "stand alones". You do *not* read them in any particular order. So.....................if you liked CHS, explore the rest of the series:

Book 1 - LOVE ON THE RUN

Book 2 – HURRICANE MEGAN

Book 3 – THE ROMANCE EQUATION

Check out www.dianeculverbooks.com for either an e-reader copy or a printed book. (NOTE: All books are available in LARGE print) A lot is planned in the future where the author tells the tales of the remaining members of the Hallock Clan. Come join the fun of living and loving in the Hamptons!

VERY SPECIAL THANK YOUS

Author assistant – Jessica Lewis is responsible for all the formatting of the books and sees them to publication. She creates the author's publicity posters, post cards and bookmarks needed for book signings. You can contact Jessica at www.authorslifesaver.com. She has designed the covers for Books 1, 2 and 3 and collaborated with the cover artist for this book. If you are an author, you need Jessica in your life!

Cover Photographer – One day as I was scrolling through Facebook, I discovered photos of my hometown of Westhampton Beach, as well as pictures of the surrounding areas of Eastern Long Island. That's when Robert Seifert and I became good "friends". When I spied the photo of the Montauk Lighthouse shown on this cover, I could not believe my good fortune that Rob would allow me to use it.

Robert Seifert is a graduate of the New York Institute of Technology and holds a Bachelor of Science in Advertising and a Master of Arts in Communication Arts. He has over 25 years of professional experience as a graphic artist, and has worked as a creative director for the majority of this time. His passion for photography was a natural progression given his appreciation of the outdoors, and, more specifically, the unique and picturesque landscape of Long Island. His work has a photographic style that is a cross between fine art and photography. The end result yields images that have a painterly mood to them yet retain all of the detail of high-resolution photography. A husband and father of two, Rob has lived on the south shore of Long Island since childhood. He enjoys spending summer weekends at the beach with his family and swimming in the ocean and bays. He can be found year-round hiking around Long Island – always with camera in hand. Check out www.robertseifertphotography.com, www.robertseifert.pixels.com, or email him at photos@robertseifert. com.

Christmas, Hamptons' Style was edited by William Coughlin. Bill Coughlin taught English and Theatre for 35 years on both the high school and college levels. He holds a MS in English/ Education from Nazareth College and a MFA in Acting from Brooklyn College. He has also worked as a professional actor in New York City and Syracuse, New York. Currently he resides outside of Syracuse with his wife of forty years, Michele. He is the proud father of two children, Alexia and Andrew. Now retired from teaching, he has found more time for his love of running half marathons, cooking, and golf.

ECKART'S LUNCHEONETTE*

You can come "home" to Westhampton Beach, walk Main Street, and put your feet in the surf, but nothing compares to eating your breakfast or lunch at Eckart's Luncheonette on Mill Road. Bought in 1911 by Jacob Eckart, a bartender, the establishment was first named the Outside Inn due to shingles hanging on the inside walls. During Prohibition in the 1920's, the family transformed the bar into a luncheonette. To this day, it is the daily place to meet for breakfast for many of the WHB natives. (Note: Before entering, there is a pecking order of those who can sit at the counter come breakfast!) Entering to have breakfast with my brother, I still see "Red", Jacob's son, standing behind the counter, a white apron wrapped around his waist. His smile lit up the room as he served up root beer floats to the teenagers stopping by after school let out. Eckart's is not only known for the smells of great food wafting through the air, but the ambiance that transports you back in time: tin ceilings, old soda jerk handles, and a root beer barrel surrounded by antique bottles. A magazine rack is filled with old magazines and newspapers telling the tales of history, both local and national, of days gone by. Even the original cash register sits atop the old phone booth. Shirley, Red's widow, has passed the torch of running the establishment to her daughter, Dee McClain. May Dee and her husband keep our historical landmark up and running for many more years to come.

*This article was first printed in Hamptons Bridge and is now reprinted with permission from Mike Domino. Laurie Culver Bumpus, a native of Westhampton Beach and the author of this book wrote the article.

ABOUT THE AUTHOR

Diane Culver wanted to write the great American novel since she was twelve. Growing up in the Hamptons during the 60's and 70's (sans paparazzi) allowed her to meet, greet and work up close and personal with many of the rich and famous. Twenty-one years later, with college diploma in hand, the real world beckoned. For the next thirty-one plus years, Diane had an award-winning career as a high school mathematics teacher, married, and raised a household of men.

One day desperately needing retail therapy, she discovered the Harlequin aisle of the local super market. A book called **Irish Thoroughbred** by Nora Roberts caught her eye. Every two weeks she squirreled away extra money to buy a new romance book. After suffering a serious health issue at the age of forty-nine, her friend and best-selling author, Gayle Callen, introduced her to a romance writers' group. Diane's dream of writing was reborn.

What does she do in her down time? She loves to travel London, Paris, and D.C. top her list. There's a bucket list of places still to go. Diane's favorite author is Jane Austen and loves to read any sequel related to P&P. She devours books on the Revolutionary and Civil War as well.

Now retired and living outside Syracuse, NY, she is probably the only person who stays inside all winter. Why freeze one's butt off? Give her a cup of Earl Grey tea, perhaps with a touch of Baileys, a fireplace glowing, and you will find her writing the next book in her series, ***Hampton Thoroughbreds***. Check out her website: www.dianeculverbooks.com or contact her at dianeculverbooks@gmail.com.

Made in United States
Orlando, FL
27 July 2022